"You're sweet to say that," he whispered.

Jared's gaze softened and dipped to her mouth.

She was locked in on him, unable to look away, though every bone in her body warned her to step back, to finish her chores and forget about how much she liked this deadly handsome, blue-eyed man standing so close. "You think I'm sweet?"

Jared's lips twitched. "And talented and smart and so beautiful I can hardly pretend not to notice."

"Jared." Was she warning him away or simply sighing his name? She was dizzy from his nearness and unable to figure any of this out.

"Bella, you're my angel." He touched a strand of her hair then, a gleam in his eyes filled with admiration and maybe something more.

"I'm no angel," she whispered.

"To me, you are."

* * *

Heart of a Texan is part of
Harlequin Desire's #1 bestselling series,

Billionaires and Babies:
Powerful men...wrapped around
their babies' little fingers.

Dear Reader,

An heiress on the run, a man's life saved and an adorable baby girl = my August release, *Heart of a Texan*!

It's been said to write what you love, what you know. And the two things I know and love are babies and food. For more than twenty years, I taught parenting and baby care at my local hospital, and that rewarding experience will stay forever close to my heart.

As far as food goes, I love it. Too much. I watch cooking shows all the time and often try the recipes that intrigue me. In *Heart of a Texan*, I decided to write about Bella Reid, Forte Food heiress on the run with her baby girl, Sienna, and the man she comes to save from a horrific car accident. Wealthy danger seeker Jared Stone isn't looking for love or a family, but Bella has now hired out as his personal chef, and their late-night cooking encounters give a whole new meaning to midnight snacks!

Take the journey with me to Stone Ridge Ranch, a place where secrets are kept and hearts collide.

If you haven't read Cooper Stone's story yet, you can find *The Texan's Wedding Escape* online, too.

Happy reading, my friends!

Charlene Sands

CHARLENE SANDS

———

HEART OF A TEXAN

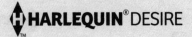

Recycling programs
for this product may
not exist in your area.

ISBN-13: 978-1-335-97165-4

Heart of a Texan

Printed in U.S.A.

™ www.Harlequin.com

Charlene Sands is a *USA TODAY* bestselling author of more than forty romance novels. She writes sensual contemporary romances and stories of the Old West. When not writing, Charlene enjoys sunny Pacific beaches, great coffee, reading books from her favorite authors and spending time with her family. You can find her on Facebook and Twitter, write her at PO Box 4883, West Hills, CA 91308, or sign up for her newsletter for fun blogs and ongoing contests at charlenesands.com.

Books by Charlene Sands

Harlequin Desire

Moonlight Beach Bachelors

Her Forbidden Cowboy
The Billionaire's Daddy Test
One Secret Night, One Secret Baby
Twins for the Texan

The Slades of Sunset Ranch

Sunset Surrender
Sunset Seduction
The Secret Heir of Sunset Ranch
Redeeming the CEO Cowboy

Heart of Stone

The Texan's Wedding Escape
Heart of a Texan

Visit her Author Profile page at Harlequin.com, or charlenesands.com, for more titles.

To my sweet daughter Nikki,
you are an amazing mother of
two precious daughters. Every day you
make us proud with your abundance
of love and kindness.

One

Francesca Isabella Forte was hiding out. Not from an evil stalker, an old boyfriend or even a shady loan shark. No, that would be too simple. It was her father. During their last argument, he'd been so furious with her, he'd disowned her. Out-and-out cut her off without a dime. Even worse, he'd threatened to take custody of her child. All because she didn't want to marry a man he'd chosen for her and she didn't want to run the Forte Foods empire.

So she'd packed up her belongings and headed straight out of San Francisco's elite Pacific Heights' neighborhood to Dallas. Using her middle name, shortened to Bella, and her married name of Reid, to all the world, she was just a young unemployed widow. Her best friend from college, Amelia Gray, had taken her in, no questions asked.

Now, Bella drove along the interstate in her rented Ford Focus, noting how different the flat Texas landscape was from her hilly hometown.

And Bella felt free.

"Hey, Bella," Amy said. "What did Cinderella say when her photos didn't show up?"

"Uh…someday my prints will come."

They giggled at the silliness and then Bella put a shushing finger to her lips. She didn't want to wake the love of her life, her twenty-two-month-old baby, Sienna, who slept peacefully in the car seat behind her.

Everyone said Sienna was the exact replica of her mommy, with shiny dark hair curling at the tips and pretty meadow-green eyes. Bella ate those compliments up, but always reminded people that Sienna was also bright, and sweet, and kindhearted, and she'd gotten all those traits from her father.

Sienna was the best thing she and Paul had ever done in their lives.

That's why she'd been so stunned when her father had threatened to sue her for custody of her baby. Marco Forte claimed she was an unfit mother. That she couldn't provide for her baby. That she'd had a mental breakdown after her husband died.

Marco had the money and influence to start the proceedings. But he couldn't do that if he couldn't find her. Her father would never get his hands on her baby. Ever.

They were fifteen miles outside Dallas proper, the road dark, the beam of her headlights the only illumination as they headed to Amy's brand-new high-rise condo. But just then a cloud of smoke billowing up from the side of the road caught Bella's eye. She blinked to make sure she was seeing correctly and, sure enough, she wasn't mistaken. A car was on fire. "Oh, no!"

She braked immediately.

"Bella, what?" Amy asked, looking up from her cell phone. "Oh, wow. You think someone's in there?"

Bella froze. Her husband's helicopter crash flashed through her mind. Paul had died on the job, in a fire just like this one, while returning from an aerial excursion in the Bay Area that he gave to tourists. She'd lost her husband; Sienna had lost her father. It had been a year ago and she still couldn't believe he was gone.

Paul, I'm so sorry.

Popping sounds from the burning car shook her out of her own head. She had no time for self-pity. She needed to do something. She couldn't just sit there. And finally it all registered.

"Amy, watch Sienna. I've got to check it out. Someone might be in that car."

God, she hoped not.

Amy blinked her eyes as if making up her mind about something. "I'll go."

"No. I have to do this myself." She couldn't explain it, but a force was driving her on. Something told her she needed to be the one to check out that car. "Please, just watch my baby."

"Okay, but be careful and don't worry about Sienna."

"I'll be careful," she said, already out of her seat belt. She could hardly believe this was happening. But she had to go. She couldn't sit back and wait for help to arrive.

She *was* the help.

If someone had gotten to Paul in time, maybe he would've survived to see his baby take her first steps, to hear her beautiful babble that was beginning to sound like real words.

Bella's feet tapped the ground lightly as she raced as fast as she could. The car must've spun off the road at high speed; it was a good ten yards off the shoulder. By the time she reached it, she was out of breath. The vehicle was overturned and someone was sitting upside down at the wheel. A man. He wasn't moving.

She whispered a silent prayer. She needed as much help as she could get. "Amy, call 9-1-1," she shouted.

"Okay!" Amy shouted back. "I'm calling now!"

The fire hadn't reached the front seat yet; at the moment, the hot flames were still confined to the engine. Was she crazy to think she could pull the man out? Probably, but she had to try. The smoke was thick, burning her nostrils, blurring her eyes. She wiped at them and took the biggest breath she'd ever taken, filling up her lungs.

The door refused to budge no matter how hard she tried. Breaking the window was her only option. She wrestled herself out of her hooded jacket and wrapped it around her fist. She'd seen this done countless times in movies and hoped it really worked. Then she squeezed her eyes closed, hauled her arm back and punched the window with all of her strength. The window shattered and crumbled into tiny pieces, like broken ice crystals.

She shook out her hand. It throbbed like crazy. She'd have to deal with that later.

Still praying, she wedged herself into the window and frantically used her fingers to find the button for the seat belt. It was strange working inside the flipped car, but finally she pressed her thumb down hard on the buckle button and the belt released. The man fell onto her like deadweight. God, he was heavy. Too late, she realized the belt had been preventing him from falling and now he was crushing her. A grunt rose from her chest as she strained to grab hold of his arms and pull him rather gracelessly out the window. He was cumbersome and it was awkward, but finally she yanked him free of the car.

Wonder Woman would've been proud.

The man's face was bloodied and bruised, yet even through all that she could tell he was handsome and young. He couldn't be much older than Paul had been when he'd died.

Only, this man wouldn't die today. Not if she had anything to say about it.

The heat was unbearable. She had to get him away from the fire. The car could blow at any second. She grabbed his arms and dragged the man closer and closer to the road, falling a few times, scraping her hands and legs over the bumpy terrain. She did her best to keep his head from further injury. Using every ounce of her strength, she finally made it a safe distance away. She gave a quick glance at the car; she could tell the blaze was traveling toward the gas tank. She held her breath and prayed. And then boom! The explosion echoed on the empty road, the blast like a rocket in flight. She sat back on her butt, immobilized as she watched the car go up in smoke.

"Oh, my God," Amy shouted. "Are you okay, Bella?"

She nodded and yelled back, "I'm not hurt. But he is."

"Paramedics are on the way!" Amy remained close to the car. Hopefully, baby Sienna was still asleep in the back seat. The little one was a great sleeper.

Bella got a grip then and looked down at the man she'd pulled from those flames. He would've died in that fire. Her body began to tremble uncontrollably.

She heard the faint sound of sirens off in the distance and her shoulders relaxed slightly in relief. But she had more to do. She couldn't wait. In this case, every second counted. This man wasn't conscious and she was pretty sure he wasn't breathing.

She knelt by his side, thankful for the summer lifeguard camp she'd attended as a teen.

I know CPR and I can help.

The scent of soot burned in Jared Stone's nostrils, putrid and strong. It felt like a big rig was sitting on his chest, making it damn hard to breathe. And something powerful hammered in his head. Everything ached and the hurt was wicked. He couldn't open his eyes. He probed his mind for clarity and…nothing. He was looping through a black hole of emptiness. What in hell had happened to him?

The last thing he remembered was driving along the highway and…

He searched and searched, straining to recall something, anything. His cell phone beeped and the beeping continued to drone in his ears. The sound grated on his nerves and then it hit him. It wasn't a phone at all. He fought to open his eyes but lost that battle. His eyes fluttered like a baby bird's but ultimately remained shut.

And then a delicate hand covered his. So soft, so gentle. The single touch comforted him in inexplicable ways, soothing his distress, taking away some of the pain. He'd never felt anything softer or more welcome. His skin responded immediately to those fingertips, feeling life again, feeling brightness where there had been only darkness.

"You're going to be all right." A woman's lilting, angelic voice seeped inside him, her tone as sweet, as memorable, as the hand that still held his. It hurt to move and his eyes wouldn't open, but that gentle voice gave him hope. Actually more than hope: *he believed her*. That serene voice wouldn't lead him astray.

"You've had an accident. I rode with you in the ambulance and now you're in the hospital. They are taking very good care of you."

He was relieved to know an angel sat by his side. Who was she? He had no clue, but she'd been with him at the accident scene and, man, he wished he could remember what had happened. The incessant beeping rang in his ears. Now he knew he was hooked up to a monitor and those beeps meant breath and heartbeats and all good things.

Jared remembered being attached to wires on a hospital machine once, after he'd been tossed off a wild stallion on the ranch. His father had told him not to go near that horse, but the daredevil in him had decided dear ole dad was being overprotective. And at the age of twelve, he took on that wild stallion and…lost. Nearly broke his neck trying to tame Balboa. He'd been unconscious for a little while, but he'd wound up walking away from that ordeal with big purple bruises all over his body, a slight concussion and wounded pride.

His dad had sold Balboa the very next day.

That had hurt more than his injuries.

Now, Jared tried to acknowledge the woman with the melodious voice by nodding his head. But the dizziness it caused shut down his attempt.

"Don't worry," she said softly. "I won't leave you. I'm here for as long as you need me to be. You were very lucky."

He didn't feel lucky. Every movement he made caused some sort of pain. But he clung to the angel's words.

I'm lucky.
I'm lucky.
I'm lucky.

Bella opened her eyes as thin streams of sunlight filled the hospital room. She'd asked for permission to visit the patient last night and the staff had been lenient, letting her since she'd saved his life. But she had fallen asleep in the chair by his bed at some point. Stretching out her arms and gently swiveling her head back and forth on her shoulders helped remove the kinks. She rose, ran her hand through her long hair and stopped midway when a thick wad of gauze got stuck in the strands. The right hand she'd used as a battering ram last night was bandaged past the wrist and partway up the arm. She'd almost forgotten how she'd broken that window to drag the man to safety.

She was certain everything underneath the bandage was bloodied and black and blue. She wiggled her fingers and felt the blood return to them, but she was pretty sure her knuckles would never be the same. It was a small price to pay. Last night the nurses had made a big fuss, insisting she have her hand x-rayed. They'd found out the patient lying in the bed nearby wasn't the only one who'd gotten lucky last night. Her hand was not broken. Hallelujah!

She grabbed her cell with her left hand and read a text from Amy.

Sienna is sleeping soundly. Not to worry.

Her baby was in good hands. Amy loved her dearly and Sienna was smitten with her mommy's best friend.

After the paramedics showed up at the accident scene, Bella had taken one look at the patient lying on the gurney and decided the man whose life she'd just saved wasn't going to the hospital alone. He had to know someone was there for him. When Paul died, he'd taken his last breaths alone. It had gutted her.

She'd asked Amy to put Sienna to bed for her. Her baby was a solid sleeper. Thankfully she hadn't inherited her mother's insomnia.

Now, in the light of a new day, she studied the man lying still on the bed. His forehead was bandaged, as were both arms. She'd overheard talk of broken ribs. She hoped the chest compressions she'd given him hadn't caused the damage. She hadn't heard or felt any break-age, but then she'd only been focused on getting the man to safety. All else had sort of blurred in her mind. Tests done last night showed no sign of internal bleed-ing. That news was gratifying. He would survive the terrible crash without any permanent damage. And, the nurse had assured her, no matter the broken ribs, her fast action had saved his life.

The man was handsome, almost to a fault. The dark bruises under his eyes and along his chin did nothing to hamper how striking he was. His jawline was angu-lar and strong, covered by a light dusting of dark blond scruff. He was tall and lean, his arms muscular.

Just then, the patient moved, rustling the bedsheets. Her breath caught in her throat as his eyes fluttered open. Eyes that were intense and captivating and ocean blue. Eyes that at the moment appeared completely con-fused.

"Hello," she whispered. "I'm glad to see you're awake."

"You're the angel," he said, his voice weak and barely audible.

She smiled and shook her head. "I'm…not an angel. I'm very real. And happy to see you're better."

He winced and pain reflected in his eyes. "Not sure about better," he whispered. "Feels like I was hit by a bus."

"Well, I didn't see a bus. But something like that."

"What happened to me?"

"I'm not sure," she said. "I was driving along the interstate and saw your car in flames quite a distance from—"

"Jared, my God. You had us scared half to death." A blond man strode into the room looking too much like the patient not to be related. Up until this point, she had no idea of his name; the hospital wasn't sharing that information.

But…Jared? That was a good name for a strong man. It fit.

The man walked straight up to Jared, looking like he wanted to crush the patient tight in an embrace and at the same time rip him a new one. "Hey, bro."

"Yeah, hey, bro."

The man peered at the bandages covering Jared's body and shook his head, tears welling in his eyes. It was a touching scene and she felt like an outsider. She was ready to slip out of the room now that Jared had his brother here to look after him. "Sorry I wasn't here sooner. The authorities had trouble tracking me down. But, man, you almost died last night. You have no idea how close you came to buying the farm." He inhaled and paused, as if regrouping his emotions. "Are you in a lot of pain?"

Jared nodded gingerly. The movement was probably too much for him right now.

"You have two broken ribs and some contusions, but honestly, bro, if it wasn't for this young lady, you wouldn't be here right now." He turned to her and put out his hand, finally acknowledging her presence. "I'm Cooper Stone. Jared's brother."

"I'm...Bella." She gave him her uninjured hand.

"I understand you pulled my brother out of the car and got him to safety."

She nodded.

"And the car was on fire at the time?"

She nodded again.

"Thank you. You were very brave," he said, his eyes misting up again. "And you were injured, too." He glanced at the bandage on her right hand.

"It's nothing. Just some scrapes."

"You did that?" Jared's voice was a little stronger now. It contained a hint of disbelief. "You pulled me out of the car?"

She understood his surprise. She stood five feet five inches tall and wore a size five dress. Hardly a match for such a big man. "How?" he mumbled.

She shrugged, her face warming from Cooper's and Jared's awed expressions. She couldn't go into the whole Paul thing or the fact that she couldn't have left him to die in that car without trying to help. Her conscience wouldn't have allowed it. "Protein, every day."

Cooper smiled.

Jared tried to smile, too, but pain seemed to grip him and he frowned instead. "Thank you," he managed.

"I'd better let the nurses know you're awake," Cooper said. "Excuse me for a second."

Bella waited until he was gone before walking over to Jared. His eyes were clear and locked on her. Having his full attention gave her the good kind of chills, and she ignored them because the bond she had with Jared Stone would be broken now. He no longer needed her.

She covered her hand with his, careful not to cause him further pain, and gave him a smile. "I'm glad I was able to help you." She nibbled on her lower lip, thinking of Paul and somehow feeling that she'd evened out the score, in a way. Jared Stone would survive. "But since your brother's here…well, I'll be leaving you in good hands."

"You stayed because I had no one else." It was a statement not a question.

"Yes, and to make sure you'd survive."

"I did, thanks to you." He applied pressure to her hand, the squeeze only slight but enough to convey his emotions. Fatigue pulled the lines of his face down and his eyes began to close.

"I'll be going now. Have a good life, Jared."

She wasn't sure if he'd heard her goodbye. Yet when she walked out of his hospital room, an odd sensation stirred in her belly. As she approached the nurses' station, she noticed Cooper in a discussion with a floor nurse.

Looking out the window, she saw a news van from a local Dallas station pulling up to the hospital. It wouldn't do to be here when the journalists started doing interviews. She couldn't afford to be recognized. She slipped past Cooper without being noticed and then exited the hospital.

Two

Sienna sat in the middle of Amy's living room, stacking colorful plastic blocks on top of each other. "I make castle," she announced.

"It's beautiful," Bella said. The formation tilted far to the left, and as soon as Sienna's chunky little hand attached the last block—shaped like a blond-haired princess—the whole thing toppled over.

Sienna broke out in giggles and Bella laughed along with her. "Oh, no!"

"Do again, Mommy. Do again." Sienna's wide green eyes beseeched her.

"Okay, sweet baby. We'll do it again."

Bella took a seat beside her daughter on the floor and helped gather up the blocks.

Amy came out of her bedroom and plopped down

on the sofa. Her home was the epitome of class and elegance, with its white furniture, glass fixtures and beautiful light-slate flooring. Amy had worked hard since their days at Berkeley, becoming a successful real estate agent. Bella could fit her small rental home where she'd lived with Paul twice over into this big luxurious condo. Yet, she'd never minded living on Paul's salary alone. Her father's form of punishment in withholding her funds had backfired on him. She'd actually loved living on a budget, as long as she and Paul were together.

"No luck on that job interview, I'm afraid," Bella told her, grabbing a few blocks and starting to build again. "I won't be the new sous chef at the Onion Slice."

"Did you do as I said?"

She shook her head. "No, I didn't cover up my bruises with makeup. It wouldn't have worked anyway. They would've seen right through it. Literally."

"I bet you didn't tell them the truth, either. That you got those scrapes from saving a man's life two days ago."

"The subject didn't come up."

"You're too modest."

"I just don't see how telling them about the accident has anything to do with my culinary skills. If they don't think I'm qualified for the job, then I'll find someplace that does. I have another interview tomorrow." She placed a pink block over Sienna's lavender one.

"Good for you. With Christmas coming, I'm sure the restaurants are busier than usual. You'll find something. But you know you can stay here as long as you like. I love having Sienna and you here for as long as it takes. Makes this big place feel more homey."

"I do know that. You've been wonderful. But I need a job. I need to get back on my feet." What she really wanted was to open a restaurant of her own. She'd worked toward that goal for a while. Now that dream had to be put on hold until she could make sense of her life.

"Have you heard any news of your father at all?"

"No, thank goodness. I didn't leave a forwarding address with anyone I know in San Francisco and I have a new cell number. Your place is so brand-new that even if he wanted to find me through you, he wouldn't be able to. He's a stubborn old mule. And Yvonne is no help. She's probably grinning from ear to ear that we're out of Marco's life now."

"The evil stepmother."

"Hardly a mother. She's only thirty-eight, ten years older than me. The thought of that woman ever raising my daughter makes me sick to my stomach."

"Your dad would never take Sienna away from you," Amy said. "It's an idle threat, Bella."

"I don't know that for sure. He was eager to accuse me of having a mental breakdown when Paul died. I did my best to hang tough, but it was difficult for me."

"You were grieving. That doesn't make you unstable," Amy said. "And you bounced back, for Sienna's sake."

A sigh blew from Bella's lips. "We're better off now. Starting fresh. Starting over. At least I won't have to worry about Dad announcing my *engagement* in the society page to a man I'd barely dated. That was the last straw."

"That was pretty underhanded," Amy said, lifting up the *Dallas Tribune*. "But it seems like you made the newspapers again, Bella. I found this last night on page three and thought maybe you'd like to see it."

Amy handed her the newspaper. The black-and-white photo of the accident scene jumped out at her first. It pictured what was left of the hot red Lamborghini and next to it was an image of Jared Stone. She skimmed the article, learning that the victim was an entrepreneur and rancher who lived on Stone Ridge Ranch quite a few miles outside the city limits. It went on to say that Jared Stone had multiple holdings and companies in and around the Dallas area and shared his ranching business with his brother, Cooper. The piece hinted at a privileged lifestyle, portraying a man who courted danger with fast cars, racing boats and motorcycles.

"Seems like your guy *has a need for speed*," Amy said, grinning.

"Yeah, well. Hopefully he's learned his lesson. When I think about what could've happened to him, I get flustered."

"Oh, yeah, that was a pretty gruesome scene. But you pulled it off. That guy doesn't know how darn lucky he was that you were driving on that road at that exact moment. There's a mention of you in there, but they didn't print your name. You're the brave mysterious woman who pulled him to safety and saved his life."

"Yeah, well, I ducked out of the hospital before the news crew arrived, I guess." She tossed the newspaper aside. "I don't want to think about it anymore. I have enough trouble sleeping at night."

"Oh, man, Bella. I'm sorry. I didn't realize it was keeping you up."

"It's nothing new. I'm a terrible sleeper. I envy people who can lay their heads down and fall asleep. That's so not me."

She helped Sienna put the princess block on the very top of the castle and this time it didn't topple over. "Yay! You did it!" She clapped her hands and Sienna mimicked her.

"I did it, Mommy!"

She hugged the baby to her chest. Sienna was growing up way too fast. She deserved a good life in a place she could call home, with a dog or a cat or a goldfish, and a backyard instead of a high-rise elevator.

But for now, they had to make do living in Dallas.

Jared leaned against Cooper, his brother bracing him under the arm as they strode into the house. He was banged up pretty badly, but after two days in the hospital, he refused to enter his home in a wheelchair. He'd make it under his own power, with a little help from Coop, and that was that.

"Man, I wish like hell you would've let me take you to my place," Cooper said for the tenth time. "Lauren is a great nurse."

"Your new bride is also pregnant. She doesn't need me underfoot and neither do you. Besides, I'll be more comfortable here." The last thing he wanted was to be a burden to the honeymooners.

Jared's home was on Stone Ridge land, a good half mile from Cooper's place. They shared the stables and pastures and got along that way just fine. They were brothers and business partners, but they both needed their own space. "You can barely walk. And even if Marie could help you around the house, she's getting too old to keep up with everything. It's not fair to her."

"Don't argue with me, Coop. It's hard enough just to breathe with these cracked ribs, much less get in a pissing match with you."

"Fine, but think about Marie."

Their housekeeper shared duties between the two houses, splitting her time between both. Jared's injuries would make it much harder for her to keep up. "Don't worry. I won't let Marie tax herself. I'll think of something."

They left the foyer and Jared gestured toward the great room, wincing slightly. "Just help me to the chair."

His favorite leather armchair faced the back window, where he had a view of the vast amount of land he called his backyard. His home was modern in most respects, but this room with throw rugs over hardwood flooring and a massive flat-screen television was more lived in, a place he could unwind and not worry about disrupting the fine order of things.

With Cooper still supporting him, Jared slowly lowered himself into the chair. He felt a sharp jolt in his chest and it took a good few seconds before the ache subsided. "I'm…okay," he said breathlessly.

Cooper's lips pulled down in a stern expression.

"You look like Dad when you do that," Jared whispered.

"And you look like a man who's...in pain."

"Good observation. Sit a minute, will you?"

Cooper took a seat on a matching leather sofa facing him.

"Tell me about the woman." The angel, whose voice calmed him, whose touch gave him solace when he might've panicked. The angel who'd risked her life to save his.

Cooper immediately knew what he was asking. "The nurses told me her name is Bella Reid. She was driving on the interstate with her friend and saw the car catch on fire. Her friend called 9-1-1 and Bella rushed over to get you out of the car before..." Cooper let out a noisy breath. "You know."

Jared gave a tiny nod. He was aware of his limitations right now, what he could and couldn't do. Mostly, he couldn't do anything, but a nod he could manage. "I can't stop thinking about it."

"Are you having nightmares?"

Jared blinked. "No. I can't remember anything about the crash. Or after, really. Except that Bella was there, holding my hand, saying all the right things to keep me calm. I need to thank her properly. See how she's doing."

"She slipped out of the hospital after I showed up, Jared. I didn't get her number. I have no way to find her. Maybe you should let it go."

"No," he said forcefully enough for Cooper's eyes to snap up to meet his. "I need to see her, Coop. My

God, that woman saved my life. I need to talk to her. Just once. I can't let it go."

"What do you want me to do, ask the sheriff to give me private information. Or how about I hire a detective?"

Jared's lips quirked up. "Nothing that drastic. You have a wife. And she's a nurse. And if she happened to see Bella Reid's medical chart…"

"I can't ask Lauren to do that."

"You don't have to. I will. She owes me a favor."

"Paul, what am I going to do?" Bella mumbled under her breath, staring at the phone in her hand. She'd just hung up with the Beaumont Club. They'd needed a chef and she'd been a day late and a dollar short. They'd just called to inform her the job she hadn't even had a chance to interview for had been filled.

Whenever she needed guidance, she'd talk to her husband. If anyone heard her, they would understand. She was a widow with a beautiful child to raise, a woman whose heart was broken the day that helicopter crashed, and she liked to think that Paul was listening to her. That he would somehow see how hard she was trying.

Her dream of working as a chef in some capacity was slowly fading.

Yesterday she'd seen an ad online for a dental receptionist. Maybe she should apply for that. The salary wouldn't buy her a house, or rent her an apartment, but it would allow her some financial independence.

Her shoulders sagging, she walked in to check on Sienna. Her baby was napping peacefully, her little olive-skinned cheeks rosy at the moment. Bella was ready to slide in next to her child on the tiny bed and try to catch a nap.

If only.

She was still debating that, watching Sienna's chest rise and fall rhythmically, when someone buzzed from the lobby. She pushed the button before it buzzed twice. "Yes?"

"It's Cooper Stone. I'd like to speak to Bella Reid."

"This is Bella."

"May I come up to see you?"

Bella leaned her shoulder against the door. "What is it? Is everything all right with your brother?"

"That's what I want to speak to you about. I promise it'll only take a minute."

Her curiosity more than anything had her beeping him in. "Come up."

"Thanks," he said.

And just a few minutes later she was showing Cooper Stone to the sofa in Amy's living room.

"Hi," he said, taking off his black cowboy hat as soon as he sat down. Bella sort of loved that about Texans. They wore hats like other people wore shoes. And only took them off when absolutely necessary.

"Hello, Cooper." She sat, too. "I have to admit I'm a little bit shocked that you're here. How did you find me?"

"Don't be frightened," Cooper said sincerely. "It's nothing bad. It's just that my brother—"

"What about Jared?" She had a vested interest in his well-being and was anxious to hear about his recovery.

It was sort of strange how she'd bonded with the person whose life she'd saved. She'd only been with him a few short hours, yet images of that night popped in and out of her mind at all times of the day and night. Thoughts of his health nagged at her.

"He's doing as well as can be expected," his brother said. "He's young and strong and he'll heal eventually."

"I see. That's good news. So then why are you here?"

"It's just that—" Cooper scrubbed a hand over his jaw "—he can't seem to get you off his mind. He wasn't all too coherent that first night and he can barely remember you at the hospital and…well…I think he needs to see you and thank you personally. It's important to him."

"I, uh, understand, but that's not really necessary."

"It is to him," Cooper said, his face somber. "Believe me, if it wasn't I wouldn't be here right now."

"You still haven't told me how you found me."

Cooper's mouth twisted and he let out a deep sigh, making it obvious he didn't want to divulge the information. "My wife…is a nurse."

He didn't have to say more. Though she was surprised that her personal contact information had been breached, she wasn't angry. She should be, but she just plain wasn't. Cooper wasn't there for nefarious reasons. He was there on behalf of his brother, who could've died a few days ago.

"Lauren, my wife, is a good woman," he began, "and she loves Jared, too. It took a lot of arm-twisting, if that makes you feel any better. I hope you'll consider coming to the ranch to see my brother. I can drive you myself or I can send a car for you."

Suddenly, Sienna ambled into the room, her soft black hair mussed. She clutched her stuffed bunny rabbit in one hand and rubbed her eyes with the other. "Hi, baby girl. Did you have a nice nap?"

Her child eyed the stranger cautiously, making a wide berth around him to get to her mommy. Bella knew the look; her daughter was wary and shy of strangers. She considered that a good thing and picked her up. Immediately, Sienna buried her face in her chest. "Sorry, she's a bit shy."

"She's adorable," Cooper said, a twinkle in his eye. "My wife, Lauren, is pregnant. Our baby is due in early spring."

Lauren, the wife who'd rifled through her personal files. "Congratulations. It's exciting. Is this your first?"

He nodded. "Yep, it's our first. How about you? Do you have any other children?"

"No, my husband died last year. It's just the two of us."

"I'm sorry to hear that. Must be hard being a single mother."

"It is. But I have great friends who help out. Amy, the woman who was with me the night of the accident, is letting us stay here until I can find employment. She's been wonderful."

"So this isn't your home?"

"It's where we live, for the time being."

His head slanting to the right, he studied her as if puzzling something out. "What kind of work do you do?"

I'm the disowned heiress of Forte Foods. "I'm a cook. Well, a chef really, but right now, I'd sling hash in the local diner if it would pay my bills." She smiled to wipe away Cooper's concerned expression and furrowed brow. That's all she'd say on the subject.

"Mommy, I hungry." The tiny voice echoed against her chest.

"Okay, sweetie. I'll make you something to eat."

Cooper rose from his seat and grabbed his hat.

She stood and gestured to Sienna. "So now you see why I can't just pick up and come to your ranch today?"

"I do see. But please consider driving out. Soon. And bring the little one. I bet she'd love to see the horses. We're at Stone Ridge Ranch. Here's my brother's card. It has his address and phone number on it." Cooper walked over to place the card in her hand. "And thanks for not freaking out about how I found you. It went against every shred of Lauren's sense of propriety, but at the same time she agreed that the only way Jared can heal mentally from the accident is to speak to you."

"That's putting a bit of pressure on me."

Cooper's brows lifted, his face the picture of innocence. "Is it working?"

She tilted her head and admitted, "Maybe."

You've got to go. I know you're dying to. Just go and satisfy your curiosity, Bella. See the man whose life you saved.

Amy's words burned in her ears as she stood on the doorstep of Jared Stone's home. There was a chill in the air and she cradled her bundled-up daughter even tighter. Mesquite trees surrounding the property were strung with big colorful ornaments. The door she'd just knocked on a moment ago was bedecked with twin pinecone wreaths reminding her that Christmas was just weeks away.

Funny, it didn't seem like Christmas. When Paul was alive it used to be such a fun time of year. Those four Christmases she'd shared with him had been the best. Now it was something she'd have to get through. But for Sienna's sake, she was going to make it special.

Her little girl was taking in the decorations in wide-eyed wonder. She pointed at an old-fashioned red buck-board wagon decorating the grassy portion of the front yard. The bed of the wagon was filled with buckets of thriving poinsettias. "Want ride, Mommy."

"Oh, sweetie, I don't think that wagon works."

"Why?" Everything lately required an explanation. Her little one was a curious soul.

"It's kind of old."

"O-kay. Is pretty," she said, still fascinated by the wagon.

"Yes, the flowers are pretty."

So was Jared's house, which was accented with thick beams of light wood and beautiful stone siding. It was modern with rustic flair. As she'd come upon it, passing stables and barns, horses and cattle along the way, somehow she could picture Jared living here. It fit. Which was a weird thing to think, since she didn't know the man. At all.

The door opened and a sixtysomething woman greeted them. "Why, you must be Bella Reid. Come in. We've been expecting you. I'm Marie, Mr. Stone's housekeeper."

Last night, after she'd made the decision to come by, she'd called Jared but the phone call had gone straight to voice mail. At least, she'd given him fair warning she was coming and was glad the message had been received. "Hello, Marie. Nice to meet you."

"And who is this little darlin'?"

"This is my daughter, Sienna."

"She's a beautiful child." Marie didn't waste time. "Please come inside. Jared's in the other room, waiting for you. He's very glad you came by." The affection in Marie's voice was unmistakable. "And I'm tickled to meet you. You saved his life. The entire family is in your debt."

Marie stopped outside a closed door and suddenly wrapped her arms around her and Sienna and gave them a hug. "Thank you." She pulled away quickly. "Don't mind me, I'm a silly woman," she said, wiping an unshed tear from her eye. "But I just had to do that."

"No, it's fine," Bella said. "It's obvious you care about Jared."

"Since he was a boy."

"Marie?" an impatient male voice called out.

"They're here, Jared." Marie swept an arm toward the door. "You'd best go inside. I left a pitcher of lemonade and a plate of cookies on the table. I sure hope you like chocolate chip," she said to Sienna. The toddler grinned at the mention of cookies. "If you need anything else, please let me know."

"Thank you."

Marie walked off slowly and Bella caught her grimacing, placing a hand to her back as she exited.

With a bit of trepidation, she entered the room to find the tall man slowly, carefully, unbending his body and rising from his chair, his expression etched with sheer determination. But there was no masking the pain he was in. "Bella Reid?"

"Hello, Jared. Please sit down," she said softly.

His face seemed to mellow, some of the strain melting away as soon as the words were out of her mouth. He wore comfortable clothes, black sweats and a T-shirt with Stone Corp printed over a graphic of a rugged mountain peak. Their company logo, she assumed.

"After you," he said. Texas manners being what they were, she wouldn't argue. She took a seat, holding her shy daughter on her lap.

"Thank you for coming," he said, his voice low and deep and much more commanding than when he'd been in the hospital. He winced as he lowered himself down. There was a bandage draped over his left eyebrow; some reddish scrapes peeked through his dark blond stubble. His longish straight hair seemed to fall in a natural part, Brad Pitt–style. His eyes were alert, deep blue and mesmerizing, the kind of eyes it was hard to turn away from. "Is this your child?"

"Yes, this is Sienna." Her daughter wouldn't look at Jared. But it was okay. She wouldn't force the issue. "She's in a clingy stage right now."

Jared smiled. His entire face brightened and she could see the man beneath the pain now. "How old is she?"

"She's twenty-two months."

"She looks like you. And that's a compliment."

"Thank you. How are you feeling, Jared?"

"I'm breathing and alive, getting by okay. I'll probably be laid up for a couple of weeks."

"You look…much better than the last time I saw you."

"I suppose I do." Again, he smiled. "I, uh, wanted to thank you properly for what you did. No, that's not entirely true. *I needed* to thank you. You dragging me out of the car and bringing me to safety saved my life. I can't thank you enough. I don't know if I'll ever be able to repay you."

"Heavens, you don't need to," she said on a breath. "I'm just glad we were coming down that road at that particular time."

"So am I. It was a lucky day for me. All I remember of that night was a soft hand covering mine, giving me comfort and soothing the panic that was building up inside. And then you spoke and the sound of your voice was like a gentle balm, an angel's call telling me I was going to be all right."

He inhaled and his face wrinkled up in pain.

"Does it hurt to talk?"

"No. Just to breathe," he said, his eyes half twinkling.

"I'm sorry."

"Don't be. I'm Texan. You know how we are."

She smiled.

"Cooper filled me in a little about you. You're a widow. I'm sorry for your loss, Bella." He spoke with reserved respect that made it seem less like prying, less like opening up old wounds.

"Thank you. It's been a bit tough, but Sienna and I are managing."

"That's good. I understand you're between jobs right now. Is that by choice?"

"Heavens no. I've been interviewing but...well, it's not going—" She paused and shook her head. "It's not important."

"I think it is."

She blinked, gazing at his solemn face. "You do?"

"Of course I do." His gaze traveled over to Sienna, who'd begun to warm up a little. She was peeking at him through her spread little fingers.

"You don't owe me anything, Jared. Honestly." God, if he wrote her out a check, she'd be mortified. She hadn't saved his life for a reward.

"Well, the truth is, I'm thinking you can help me and I can help you."

"How?"

"You met Marie. She's a sweetheart, but she's getting on in age and my present condition is taking a toll on her with all the extra work she has to do. For years, she's worked part-time here and part-time at Cooper's place. Now I'm afraid the chores are too much for her."

"What are you saying to me? How can I help?"

"I understand you're good in the kitchen and it just so happens I'm in need of a personal chef."

She gulped air, totally surprised. "You need a personal chef?"

"Yes. I've been thinking about this for a long time.

Marie's got too many chores around here as it is. She could use the break and…well, I'm offering you the job."

"To…be…your…personal…chef?"

He smiled, his eyes lighting up again, as if he was glad she was catching on. Oh, yeah, she was. He was indebted to her and this was how he was going to repay her. "Yes."

"But, you don't even know if I'm qualified."

"You can send me a résumé at your convenience. But I don't need one. I trust you're up to speed on your cooking skills."

"Oh, yeah? And how would you know that?"

"Because…I already know what kind of person you are. Besides, I'm not fussy. Just put a burger and fries in my face and I'm happy."

She laughed. "I'll remember that."

"So you'll take the job?"

"I didn't say that. There's a lot to consider."

"You need a job and I need a cook. What's to consider?"

"You're forgetting that you live way out here, miles away from Dallas. Working out babysitting arrangements would be difficult, if not impossible. I don't want to be gone from Sienna for too long during the day."

"That's the beauty of this great big ranch house." He spread his arms wide. The gesture cost him physically. Her heart went out to him, seeing him so bravely mask his pain. "You can have your own wing of the ranch house, two rooms just for you and Sienna upstairs. I'm basically living down here right now anyway since climbing the stairs is like a *Ninja Warrior* obstacle for me. You'd have all the privacy you'll need."

"My goodness, Jared. You want us to move into your house? I mean, that's generous and all, but I can't—"

"Don't say you can't. Think about it. You'll have a job where you won't have to leave Sienna at all. She'll be right here while you're working. She'll have a yard to play in and wide-open spaces to run at her heart's content. Don't get me wrong, I'm thankful that you saved my life, but I really do need some more help here. My solution is a good one, for all of us."

He had a good heart but her pride was getting in the way of her good sense.

"I don't know…"

"Give it a try, Bella." His voice cut into her senses. So deep, so sincere. He really wanted to help her and she appreciated that. "If it doesn't work out, there'll be no hard feelings. It'll be up to you."

He was offering her something better than she could ever hope for: employment, a home and a way to stay close to Sienna. Taking the job would buy her time to sort out her life and make some long-range plans. "Let me talk it over with my best friend. I, uh, just need a little bit of time."

"It's a deal," he said and then glanced at her daughter. "Would you like a cookie, Sienna? You can have as many as your mommy says you can have."

Sienna faced him and smiled, her sweet dimples lighting up her cheeks.

"One," Bella said in her mommy tone.

"Like I said," he began, "you can have *one* cookie.

And I bet your momma would spring for some lemonade, too."

Sienna giggled, nodding at the man who could barely move on the chair opposite her.

He was in bad shape right now and seemed genuine in his job offer.

Could she take a leap of faith and accept the job? Could she go through with it, concealing her true identity from Jared Stone in order to keep Sienna safe?

Or maybe the real question was, could she afford not to take the job?

Later that night Amy plunked down on the sofa next to Bella and handed her a glass of pinot grigio. "Here, take this and sip at will. There's plenty more where that came from."

Bella stared at the wine bottle sitting on the cocktail table in front of her. She probably would need to empty it before she could come to a decision.

Amy crossed her legs under her, sinking into a conversational posture on the sofa and sipping wine. "Not that I'm trying to get rid of you but, honestly, Bella, this man is offering you a golden opportunity. Why not jump at it?"

Sienna had fallen asleep an hour ago. And this was supposed to be Bella's Zen time. Where she could find some peace in the quiet surroundings and shut her mind down a little bit. But Jared Stone's offer kept interrupting her serenity. Amy was on board with the idea, but there was still a nagging notion that wouldn't go away. "Because I know why he's offering me a job. Or *making up* a job. He sees me as the poor widow, a single mom raising a baby all by myself. It's charity."

"For one, you are all those things and more."

Bella stared at her friend.

"What I mean is, he sees you as a widow raising a child alone, but also as the courageous person who saved his life. It's *so* not charity. If he was going to hire someone—and you said it yourself, his housekeeper really seemed like she could use the help—why can't he hire you? I'd bet he'd much rather hire someone he trusts, someone who really needs the work, than a total stranger."

"I am a stranger. He didn't even want to see my résumé."

"Lucky for you, he didn't. What would you put on there? Former heiress of Forte Foods."

"I did go to culinary school, you know. Even though I didn't finish, I learned a lot and what I didn't learn I taught myself. I have been around the food industry and chefs all my life."

Amy smiled. "There, you see, you just made a great argument for yourself. You are qualified for the job. My goodness, he's one man. You could cook for him with your eyes closed."

"I'd have to move to his ranch. And I'd be deceiving him the entire time. Could I really do that?"

"For Sienna's sake, you have to. It's a darn good reason."

"I don't know."

"What don't you know? It's perfect. What do I have here for you and Sienna? Concrete and glass. My balcony is too dangerous for Sienna, so the poor kid can't even get some sunshine or breathe fresh air. Sienna would love being in a place where she could run wild. She'd be around cattle and horses. Maybe a dog or cat or two. And how long do you think it would take your father to find me, if he really wanted to? He knows we're friends. If he came looking for you, you'd be out of luck. But this way…"

"I'd be on a ranch in the middle of nowhere." Amy's arguments made sense.

"Take the leap," her friend said. "I'll be right here if it doesn't work out. You have nothing to lose."

Bella finished her pinot in one large gulp. "Okay, I'm gonna do it. I'll take the leap and call Jared Stone tomorrow."

Three

On Saturday morning, three days after meeting with Jared Stone, Bella followed a good-natured Marie up to her new rooms at Stone Ridge. The woman seemed genuinely glad to have her there. "I'll be staying today to help you get settled in," she said with a smile. "If you need anything, or have any questions, be sure to ask. Mr. Stone is down in his study. He's anxious to get back to work. If you ask me, it's too soon, but that boy is determined. He said as soon as you feel up to it, he'd like to see you."

Jared Stone had arranged for her things to be moved into the house this morning. All she'd had when she'd walked out of her father's house in Pacific Heights was a few pieces of luggage and three boxes of baby gear. She'd traveled light…well, as light as she could with a toddler in tow. Sienna had toys and special blankets and dolls that she couldn't live without. Really, Bella could have boxed it all up and placed it in her car, but her new employer had insisted on sending someone to help move her.

"Thank you, Marie. I should be down soon. As you can see, I don't have too much to unpack."

Marie's kind eyes warmed as she took in the meager boxes and suitcases on the floor.

Oh, goodness, she didn't want to give the woman the wrong impression. She didn't mean she was so destitute that these were all the things she owned in the world. Too late. Marie turned her attention to Sienna. "How's the little princess today?"

"Sienna, say hello to Marie."

Sienna wiggled her fingers in a shy wave. She didn't want to cross the cookie lady.

"She's going to have a bit of fun here on the ranch. You be sure to take her around and explore. There's a lot to see through a toddler's eyes."

"I will. Thank you."

"I'll be off now," Marie said. "Remember to ask if you have any questions. I'm just tickled as can be you're here. You two will bring some life into these four walls."

"You may get more life than either of you bargained for."

"Nonsense. Children only bring the world joy," Marie said as she made her way out of the room.

With Sienna latched onto her hip, Bella looked around the second floor of the house. Two adjoining bedrooms, both with queen-size beds, and a good-sized bathroom would be her new home. The rooms were lovely and in shades of light blues and lavenders with bleached white-oak contemporary furniture. She was pretty certain no one had ever stepped foot inside these immaculate guest quarters. Sienna would give the place a lived-in look within a matter of hours. Poor Jared Stone didn't know what he was in for, inviting a toddler almost two years old into his home. And poor her, trying to keep Sienna's antics down to a minimum. Jared didn't know it yet, but his quiet existence would soon be replaced with chaos and noise.

Bella walked over to the window and peered directly down into a backyard full of thick green grass and a flowery garden. There was a pool with a rock slide and trickling waterfall. All of the pool chairs and tables were protected and covered, but she could just imagine how inviting the pool would be on a scorching-hot Texas day. Her gaze traveled farther out to a pasture. Those tiny specks across the vista had to be a herd of cattle.

She glanced around the room again and sighed. "Well, Sienna, time to unpack our stuff."

Fifteen minutes later she'd organized the bathroom, complete with an Elmo toothbrush set, child-safe shampoo and body wash and Princess Jasmine towels. Sienna would sleep with her, until she got acclimated, and one way to do that was to put all of her toys in the second bedroom. All of their clothes combined didn't take up one-tenth of the generous walk-in closet space.

It was weird coming to live here with a total stranger, though Amy had done a thorough Google search of Jared Stone and eagerly shared that he was a successful rancher, an astute businessman and a budding entrepreneur. Recently he and his brother Cooper had funded the building of a playground for the local community. And his charitable donations didn't stop there.

He's hardly an ax murderer.

Amy's words sunk into her skull and she immediately felt better about coming to live here. "Okay, baby girl," she said. "It's time to say hello to the boss."

Taking hold of Sienna, she climbed down the stairs and went in search of the study. The house wasn't hard to figure out; it was as sprawling as a two-story ranch home could be, and after stepping into the beautiful gourmet kitchen, excitement stirred as she ogled her new "office." Sienna babbled loudly in her own sweet language as she made her way past the kitchen to the hallway leading to the study. Sienna squirmed and fussed to be let down. She had yet to have her nap. "Here you go," Bella said, setting the baby on her feet, "but please don't touch anything." She knocked on the partially shut door.

"Come in." The pitch of Jared's voice was deep and welcoming.

She opened the door and found Jared sitting behind his desk, closing down his laptop computer. Color had returned to his cheeks, his bandages were off and the scrapes on his face appeared to be healing. He wore a black snap-down shirt and jeans, looking much better than he had just three days ago.

He was handsome, there was no denying that. He now had a healthier glow about him; his eyes, less shadowed by pain, were deeper, bluer, mesmerizing.

Her heart raced. She would be living with him now, in this house, and all the awkwardness she'd felt the other day came back in full force. This would be her new normal.

He began to rise and she gestured for him not to. He did it anyway. He had to be six foot two if he was an inch. "Welcome to Stone Ridge."

"Please sit down, Mr. Stone. If you get up every time I walk into a room, you'll make yourself dizzy."

He chuckled and then his face hardened and his hand automatically went to his broken ribs. Of all his injuries, that one must be the most painful. "I will, if you call me Jared from now on."

"Okay…Jared."

"Please, take a seat."

She did, sitting opposite him. Sienna stood next to her chair, looking all around, taking in the big room with windows facing the groomed yard and books stacked on a wall of shelves. But her eyes found and stayed on two packages decorated with pastel balloon wrapping paper on the floor beside the desk.

"Hello, Sienna," he said. "I hope you'll like it here."

Sienna took one look at Jared, forgot about the packages and climbed up on Bella's lap, hanging on to her neck with a death grip. Bella pried her off her neck as gently as possible and her baby settled into a fetal position in her arms. "She'll warm up. This is all so new for her."

"I figured," he said.

"You're feeling better?" she asked.

He nodded. "Every day gets a bit easier. I should be

one hundred percent in a few weeks or so." He paused as if speaking of his injuries made him uncomfortable. "I hope you like your accommodations. If there's anything you want changed, anything you need, just let me know."

"Thank you. That's very generous of you. The rooms are lovely and we're going to manage just fine."

"Good to hear. Marie will be here today to show you around the kitchen and the rest of the property. Feel free to use anything on the ranch, including the horses, if you like to ride. And if you need something—"

"I'll be sure to ask," she said.

Jared smiled, a much easier smile than the one he'd attempted a few days ago. He wrote something down on a piece of paper and slid it over to her. "Here's your starting salary. I think it's in line with the going rate."

She glanced at the number and was relieved to see he wasn't overpaying her. "Yes, it's perfect." It was a fair sum considering she was also getting room and board. If that number was even slightly higher, she'd feel less legitimate. The salary he offered allowed her a measure of pride. And Jared Stone seemed to be sensitive to that. "Thank you."

"I don't expect you to work every day. You'll have Sundays and Mondays off, if that's okay with you."

"That's fine. I, um, have a few questions for you, though, if you don't mind?"

"I don't mind at all," he said.

She sat a little straighter in the chair; Sienna was happy as a clam to continue to cling to her. "Well, since

I'm cooking for you, I'd like to know how you see yourself food-wise."

"How do I see myself?"

"Yes. What's your culinary landscape?"

"In English, please?"

She held back a grin. "Okay. Are your food tastes conservative, traditional, adventurous, exotic, selective…"

"I'm definitely adventurous. There's nothing I won't try. Except liver. No liver, please." He made a little-boy face, scrunching up his mouth, and she laughed.

"No liver, check. Spicy?"

"Yes, but not necessarily all the time."

"Do you drink alcohol?"

"Does the sun shine?" he shot back.

She laughed. "Okay, got it."

He was basically a cook's dream. He liked to try new things and he ate everything, pretty much. She'd put that to the test very soon.

The healthy cast on his face when she'd walked in was beginning to fade. How long had he been at his desk working? She knew the look of fatigue. Being a single mom, she'd had many a sleepless night. And even when she did catch some winks, it wasn't for very long. Not all of that had to do with Sienna. She had a classic case of insomnia, an inherited trait. *Thank you, Marco.*

Too late, she averted her eyes. She'd been staring at Jared. And he'd been quietly staring back.

"If there's nothing more—"

"Actually, there is," he said.

Gingerly, he rose from his seat to full height. When standing, he was a solid presence in the room, a man who commanded attention. She'd noticed that about Cooper, too. "I have something for you both. It's a little welcome gift."

"You didn't have to do that." Goodness, she meant it. How awkward was this? What could he have possibly gotten the two of them?

"Would you like to open Sienna's first. It's in the big box."

He moved over to the two boxes by his desk. "Sienna, this is a present for you. Do you want to help your mother open it?"

Her daughter's eyes went adorably wide and she eased off her lap, took her hand and pulled her over to the wrapped box.

"Christmas isn't for a few weeks," she told Jared.

Jared only smiled.

Sienna grabbed at the paper and Bella helped her the rest of the way until all the wrapping was off. When the box was open, Jared explained. "Some assembly required."

Sienna took one look at her gift and started flapping her arms like a little bird. "Bike! Bike!"

"I can see that," Bella said.

The balance tricycle was hot pink with streamers on the handlebars and a chrome bell. It was already assembled except for the long rod that attached to the back step, so that it could be pushed and guided from behind. The training bike of tricycles.

Sienna found the bell and that was that. The ringing lasted at least thirty seconds before Bella took her hand away. "Sienna, do you like the tricycle?"

She began nodding. "Me yike it, Mommy."

"Can you say 'thank you'?"

"Tank you," she said without hesitation. Her eyes were transfixed on her new trike.

Jared grinned. "You're welcome. Now you can ride around the ranch in style."

"It's very generous of you," Bella said.

"There's a helmet for her, too. Lauren, my sister-in-law, said she couldn't ride outside the house without one."

"Yes, that's true. Again, very thoughtful."

Bella took the trike out of the box and set it on the floor. Immediately, Sienna, thrilled beyond belief, lifted her leg and tried to climb up. Bella gave her a little push and then she was all set, her butt settled on the padded seat.

"Your feet touch the pedals. Oh, my baby is getting to be such a big girl."

"I'll attach this thing," Jared said, a screwdriver suddenly appearing in his hand. He lifted the rod out and bent on his haunches. His body creaked and his face went white, but his jaw was tight, determined. Bella bent, too, and suddenly she was inches from Jared, breathing in a light musk scent, seeing the tiny lines of pain around his eyes. And for a second, the briefest of moments, she saw not the victim whose life she'd saved, but a beautiful, bone-melting, blue-eyed man.

Amy would say he was a hunk to the hundredth degree.

"Can you hold this?" he asked.

"Oh, uh, yes." She secured the rod while he screwed it to the back step of the trike.

"There," he said, his breathing labored. He was taxing himself, but there was a gleam of accomplishment in his eyes that shouldn't be shot down. "That should work."

"Yes, it's nice and tight."

"And now for your gift." He began to rise and wobbled a little. She was there immediately to catch him, putting her arm around his waist. He used his other hand to brace himself on the desk and then gazed at her. "I've got it," he said quietly, the sexiness in his voice playing tricks on her.

"Yes, you do. Sorry."

"For trying to rescue me again?"

"For—" She shrugged. "I don't know why." The words tumbled out of her mouth and, too late, she took her arm off his waist. Jared Stone definitely made her nervous.

He smiled. A killer this time, showing white teeth, handsome lines around his mouth and a twinkle in his eyes.

Sienna was patiently examining her new trike. Once again the temptation to ring the bell was too much for her and clanging filled the room. "A set of drums might've been less noisy," Bella remarked.

A chuckle rumbled from his chest, one that caught him off guard. He winced, but it was brief and soon replaced with a smile. "I'll remember that next time. This one is for you," he said, pointing to the other wrapped gift. "I'm told every chef should have a good set of these."

She stared at him for a moment and then carefully unwrapped her gift. It was an attaché case and inside she found a twenty-four-piece set of executive chef knives. They were beautiful, of the finest caliber, the handles made of rosewood.

"Oh…" A lump formed in her throat. She'd grown up with privilege and had had the finest of things, but this gift was special. It was the first time she'd been recognized as a legitimate chef. Other than by Paul. Her husband had believed in her and was awed by her talent, but her father and his wife had never taken her seriously. "It's too much. I love it but—"

"No buts. Marie told me our kitchen was sorely lacking in equipment, and you should have all the tools you need at your disposal."

"You mean for those burgers and fries I'm going to toss your way."

Jared laughed.

"Thank you. It's a beautiful set."

Sienna went for the bell again and the ringing echoed off the study walls. "Well, we'd better get out of your hair now. Do you have more work to do?"

"Actually," he said, running a hand down his face, "I'm getting hungry for lunch. I'm up early most days, so I'm usually hungry about this time."

It was a little after eleven in the morning. She made a mental note of Jared's timetable. "It's good to know. I can make up a simple lunch, if you'd like."

"No. That's not necessary. Marie's got it covered today. You can join me, or you can let the little one play on her trike."

"In the house?"

"Sure…it's fine. She can't hurt anything."

"Obviously you haven't been around a two-year-old before."

"Can't say that I have," he said good-naturedly. "But between Sienna and Cooper's kid, I'm gonna get a real fast education."

That much was very true.

She opted to let Sienna ride up and down the hallway, guiding her with the rod and praying she wouldn't take out anything super expensive in her wake.

Dawn popped its way into Jared's window much too soon to his liking. He usually wasn't a bad sleeper, but the afternoon naps he'd been taking since the accident had a way of messing up his schedule. Dr. Corona had told him to rest as much as possible, and by the middle of the day, he was too wiped out to disobey. Who knew broken ribs could cause so much grief to his body?

Feeling helpless wasn't his style. He was mentally ready to get back behind the wheel. He had a garage full of vehicles, two motorcycles and several cars, as well as a speedboat docked at the nearby lake. He wasn't about to let what happened scare him away. But he had to heal first, and all the tossing and turning during the night did nothing to help his busted-up body repair itself. Today, even if he had to pry his eyes open with miniature pitchforks, he was going to fight the nap, tooth and nail.

Slowly he hinged himself up from the bed and drew a lungful of air into a diaphragm that was tight and sore. Those first few moves after being bedridden during the night were the hardest. He managed to stand without the help of a cane. Call it ego, but he'd have to be on his last breath before he'd submit to using that thing.

He managed to get his jeans on, grunting with each tug burning straight through his rib cage. The sting lingered like an unruly drunken uncle on Christmas day.

He'd never take getting dressed for granted again. "Marie," he called out. He hoped like hell she was there. He hoped she'd heard him.

He heard the sound of footsteps approaching, down the hallway and just as he was zipping up his fly, help arrived. It was Bella. She took two steps into his room, and budding sunlight cast a circular light around her head like a halo… *His angel.*

He blinked.

And was struck by her absolute beauty. She wore white jeans and a silky jade blouse that made her soft green eyes really come alive. With all that blue-black hair cascading down her back in a braid and her face shining and free of anything unnatural, Bella made his breath hitch. His rib cage hurt like hell, but as he slowly released pent-up breaths his focus never wavered. He was totally aware of her now and a spark of excitement strummed inside him, obliterating the pain.

Why now? It wasn't as if he hadn't noticed how pretty she was before. Of course he'd noticed, but he'd never let his mind go there. She was an employee, a widow and a mother of a small child. Three very solid reasons why the thought hadn't entered his mind. But right now, in an unguarded moment, when he wasn't expecting to see her, suddenly he'd become very aware of her appeal.

Her eyes seemed stationed on his bare chest and her face colored as red as an apple, a tough feat for a woman with olive skin. He'd shocked her, no doubt, but he also witnessed a glint of admiration in her eyes.

"Jared?"

"Mornin'."

"Good morning. Do you, uh, need something? I heard you call out for Marie. She's at your brother's today. But if you need her, she told me to be sure to call her."

"No. Not necessary. Guess I forgot it was her day with Coop."

Bella looked straight into his eyes, as if she'd be set on fire if he caught her staring any longer at his chest. He could almost smile at that.

"What did you need?"

"Nothin'."

"You called for Marie for a reason."

"It's not in your job description."

She glanced at the shirt on the chair. "You need help getting your shirt on?"

There was no sense denying it. "Yes. But—"

"Heavens, if you need help with it, I can do it." She sounded slightly annoyed, as if she were scolding a child. She stepped farther into the room, picking up his shirt as she approached, keeping her eyes level with his. No more sneak peeks at his chest.

"Here you go." She held out one arm of the shirt. "We'll take it slow." Her angelic voice, soft and accommodating, came back. If only he could close his eyes and listen to her all day long.

She smelled like cookies, a sugary vanilla scent teasing his nostrils. And then he gazed at her mouth, heart-shaped and rosy-lipped. She'd given him rescue breaths with that mouth. Oh, man.

She guided his right arm into the sleeve first and scooted it up his arm as he ever so slowly pushed his arm through. "Now comes the hard part," he said.

She wound the shirt around his back and he had to stretch his left arm way out to push it through the sleeve. By the time they were through, beads of sweat trickled down his forehead.

"Maybe a T-shirt would be easier," she said, tilting her head, analyzing the situation.

"That would be a no. I tried that already."

"Are you okay?" Her green eyes held sympathy.

"I'm fine. Thank you." He sniffed the air. "Besides you, something smells wonderful out there."

"Besides me?"

He grinned. "Sorry, thinking out loud. You smell like a cookie."

An angel with a tranquil voice who smelled like cookies…good thing he had his head on straight about Bella Reid. She was a no-go. He was gun-shy anyway. He'd had his heart ripped out by Helene and some wounds just refused to heal.

"Thank you, I think," she said, standing in front of him now, keeping her eyes on the snaps she was fastening on his shirt. She stood a few inches from him and as soon as she was through took a big step back. "The drawbacks of a being around food all the time. But smelling like vanilla is much better than smelling like garlic. Or, God forbid, liver."

He smiled. "So true."

He was glad she'd moved away. He was injured but he wasn't dead. If anyone could bring a man back from the dark depths, it was Bella Reid. She'd done that literally for him once already. He wasn't going to push his luck.

"So what is that delicious smell?" he asked.

"I made apple crostata this morning."

"Already?" He had no idea what an apple crostata was, but it sure sounded good.

She nodded. "I've got it cooking in the oven for breakfast or a midmorning snack. I bake while Sienna is sleeping. I hope I didn't wake you."

"I didn't hear a thing."

"Okay, great. So would you like eggs and bacon to go with the crostata? Marie already told me how you like your coffee. It's brewing now."

"You're efficient."

"It's easy when you love what you do."

"And how long have you been doing this?"

"Oh, all of my life. I learned to cook at an early age. Out of boredom maybe, but I found I had a great passion for it. I can't imagine not doing it. Bacon and eggs?" she asked again.

"Uh, yeah. Thanks."

"Give me twenty minutes."

"Will you and Sienna be eating at the same time?"

It grated on him how much he enjoyed having a conversation with her. Her voice was permanently ingrained in his memory, and every time she spoke to him, something sweet and pleasant filled him up.

"I don't think so. Sienna sleeps until eight. It gives me time to get a few things done before my little tornado hits."

"That precious child?"

"Just wait," she said as she walked out of his room.

He smiled, watching her go. He really didn't want to eat breakfast alone.

Again.

Four

At breakfast, Bella watched Jared wipe his dish clean, soaking up the last of his soft-boiled eggs with a wedge of sourdough toast. It was gratifying to see him eat so hardily. The crostata was nearly half gone. Granted, he'd made her sit at the kitchen table and have a bite with him, so she'd had a nibble, as well.

"I'll be three hundred pounds if you keep feeding me this way," he said, plopping the last of his toast into his mouth. "What's in that crostata that makes it taste so good?"

"That's a chef's secret," she said. "But if you promise not to tell…"

"I promise."

"Butter…lots of butter. Everything tastes better with butter."

"I thought that's what they say about bacon."

She smiled. "That, too."

She got up and poured him another cup of coffee. He liked it black with one heaping spoonful of sugar. "You must not eat what you cook," he said.

"I do."

He glanced at the waistline of her white jeans and then lifted his gaze to her chest before meeting her eyes, shaking his head the entire time. "How do you do it?"

"It has something to do with chasing around a toddler. Plus I make it a habit to eat bites of food instead of the entire dish."

"Ah," he said, "that explains it." He glanced at his completely empty dish. "Guess I failed at that. But it was delicious."

"Thank you. But, Jared, just so you know, I like to balance the meals, so that you're not eating heavy at every meal. Lunch will be light, I promise."

"Because you don't want a three-hundred-pound employer?"

"Because of the *H*-word. Some chefs don't believe in it, but I do."

His brows gathered and a question formed on his lips.

"Healthy eating. Emphasis on good health."

"Does that mean I can't have beef? You do know I co-own a cattle ranch."

She smiled. "It means there are leaner cuts of meat and ways to prepare them that are healthier than others."

"I do know that."

"Until you're back on your feet, it'd be best if I keep the food on the lighter side."

"No more crostata?"

She shrugged, feeling a bit guilty. "I wanted to make a good first impression on you on my first day."

"Darlin', you don't have to worry about my impression of you. I already think you're a combination of Wonder Woman and Clara Barton."

She nibbled on her lower lip and a flush of heat raced to her cheeks. She couldn't look at him. He was too honest, too humble and too darn appealing. It made her hate herself a little bit to find him so attractive.

Images of Paul popped into her head and she quickly grabbed Jared's plate and walked it to the sink. "I think I hear Sienna. She's waking up," she said with her back to him. She wiped her hands on a dish towel. "I'll be back later to clean this up."

She moved past him, feeling Jared's striking blue eyes on her as she exited the kitchen.

Sienna was just waking up as she walked into the bedroom. The baby slept with her in the big bed, surrounded by lush pillows to protect her from falling. She was sitting up, rubbing her eyes. "Mommy."

Bella sat next to her on the bed. "Mommy's here."

The baby lunged for her and Bella's heart lurched. This little child was her life. She was dependent on her. And Bella vowed that she was going to make a good life for her. Every penny of her earnings would go into one day opening up her own restaurant. It had been a dream of hers since she was a child and it had stayed with her all this time. She wasn't the corporate type. She wasn't cut out for business. She wanted to create food, and maybe work on a cookbook one day, too. All of her lofty aspirations were for Sienna's future now.

An image of Jared in his bedroom, zipping up his pants, his chest ripped with muscles, popped into her head. He was one sexy man. A man she felt a bond to, because she'd saved his life, but a man who wasn't going to upset her dreams. She couldn't allow it.

She still loved Paul and as she hugged his child to her chest, she was immediately reminded of the love they'd shared. Sienna was a result of that love. Bella wouldn't forget that.

"Sienna, it's time for your bath. Let's get the water ready in this nice big tub." The triangular tub was set at an angle in the corner of the room. It was big enough for four children. As she filled the tub and poured in child-safe bubble bath liquid, Sienna began lifting her princess nightie over her head. "Good girl, Sienna." Bella removed her soaked diaper and then set her little naked baby into the tub.

Sienna giggled her head off, splashing her mommy immediately, just like always. The power of a smiley-faced, lovable child made all things seem possible. Bella found herself relaxing for the first time since coming to the ranch. She told herself that this might work out after all, as long as her father didn't hunt her down and ruin everything.

An hour later, after Bella had managed a quick cleanup in Jared's kitchen and had planned the lunch menu for the three of them, she stood on the stone pathway that led around the entire house. The gardens were on their last stages of pretty, the flowers fading, threatened by colder temperatures and harsher weather.

"Ready, Sienna?"

The baby sat on her new trike with a hot-pink helmet on her head, chin straps securing it in place. "Reddee, Mommy."

"Hold on tight." Sienna gripped the white handles and Bella began pushing her down the wide pathway. Sienna giggled as they moved forward, ringing the bell over and over until Bella was sure the cows in the distant pasture were covering their ears.

As they were coming back around, Jared stepped out of the house and leaned against a pillar at the top of the steps. "Uh-oh," Bella mumbled.

Jared kept his eyes focused on the two of them as Sienna tried to steer her trike. They were both getting the hang of it, but it was clear they needed more practice.

"Are we too loud?" Bella asked, coming to a standstill in his line of vision.

He shook his head. "Not at all. Just needed a breath of air."

For a man who liked going fast and being active, it was clear Jared hated being cooped up in his gorgeous house. The outdoors looked good on him.

"Don't let me stop you," he said. "Sienna's doing pretty good."

Sienna recognized his praise and smiled, her chest puffing out.

"I think so, too. She's never ridden one of these before." Bella left Sienna's trike and put herself in between

Jared and her daughter, whispering, "Um, do you think I should make the bell disappear?"

His mouth quirked and his blue eyes brightened. "Are you a magician?"

She grinned. "I can be."

"If you do, I have a feeling another bell would have to magically appear."

She blinked. "You're sure?"

He nodded. "Doesn't bother me. What would bother me is if that smile was wiped clean off Sienna's face."

Thank you, she mouthed to him, a sudden sting burning behind her eyes. She was touched by his acceptance. The two of them clearly were a disruption in his life.

A car pulled up and all heads turned as a woman in a stylish, body-hugging, neon running outfit exited the vehicle. She held a covered dish in her hands and as she approached, her eyes were all for Jared. She gave him a big smile, her cinnamon-red hair cascading down her back as she hurried up the pathway. Before Bella could scoot Sienna away and give them privacy, the woman was in front of them.

"Jared Stone, I am so glad to see you up and around. When I heard about the accident, I was worried silly about you."

Jared smiled at her. "Hello, Johnna Lee. It's good to see you."

"Same here." She walked up the steps and put one arm around his neck, giving him a gentle hug. "I made you some of my special mac and cheese. Just the way you like it, with extra breadcrumbs on top."

"That's awfully nice of you," Jared said.

She held on to the casserole dish and traded looks with Bella, waiting for an introduction.

"Uh, Johnna Willis, this is Bella Reid. She's new to Stone Ridge." Jared turned to her. "Johnna is my neighbor. She lives just up the road."

"Pleasure to meet you," Johnna said kindly. "And who's this little cutie pie?"

"This is my daughter, Sienna."

The woman bent a little and spoke directly to her daughter. "Hello, Sienna. I sure do like your tricycle."

Sienna put her face down on her handlebars.

"Sorry, it takes her a while to warm up to new people," Bella explained.

"I totally get it. I was a shy kid, too. If you can believe that." She chuckled at the thought and Bella smiled. "She's really adorable."

"Thank you."

"So what do you do here at Stone Ridge?" Johnna asked.

"I'm…" She glanced at Jared and he gave a nod. "I'm Jared's personal chef. Uh, while he's recuperating."

"Oh, I didn't know Marie finally retired."

"She didn't." Jared intervened. "I think Marie's going to outlast all of us Stones. But with my accident and all, Marie needed some help."

Johnna blinked. "Well then, that's a good thing."

The conversation could've gotten awkward, being that she went to the trouble to cook her special mac and cheese dish for Jared, yet she chose to be gracious.

"I think so. Johnna, would you like to come inside?" Jared asked.

She didn't hesitate. "I'd sure love to. I need to hear all about how you're doing."

"Excuse me, Jared," Bella said. "Would you like me to fix you all a drink?"

"No thanks. Let Sienna play," he answered. "I think I can handle this." After Johnna walked past him toward the door, he gave Bella a shrug, his gaze lingering on her a bit. It was an intimate look and she figured it had more to do with him preferring to stay outdoors than having anything to do with her.

She sighed. So Jared had a woman caller. He'd probably had many. And good for him.

Yeah, good for him.

The second the door closed, Sienna's face popped out of hiding. "Mommy, ride."

"Okay, baby. Let's go."

She had an hour before she had to start on Jared's lunch. Unless he wanted mac and cheese instead. With extra breadcrumbs.

Just the way he liked it.

Heavens, Bella. Don't be a nitwit.

After a thirty-minute visit, Jared bid farewell to Johnna. She was a friend and neighbor, but at times she pushed a little too hard, and he always tried setting her straight without hurting her feelings. It had been sweet of her to cook him a meal and to offer to help with Christmas decorating. But ever since his breakup with his ex, he'd pretty much given up on the holidays. He related Christmas to Helene. It hadn't been pretty the night he'd found out she'd betrayed him and taken him for a fool. They'd been planning a Christmas wedding before everything had blown up in his face.

This year, Marie had insisted on decorations to boost everyone's spirits. He'd had his crew get started on the exterior of the house, but he had yet to do anything inside.

His phone rang and Jared lowered himself slowly into a chair to take the call. "Hey, Coop."

"Hey. How's it going? What are you doing?"

"It's going okay. Actually, I just said goodbye to Johnna. She stopped by for a visit, brought me a dish of food."

"Nice of her. Did you tell her you have a new chef cooking in your kitchen?"

"Actually, I didn't have to. She met Bella and Sienna outside."

"How did she take it?"

"Take what?"

"Nothing, bro. Just that she's had her eyes on you for a while."

"She's just being neighborly."

"Neighborly? Is that what they're calling it these days?"

"Okay, I hear you. But I'm not interested."

"You haven't seriously dated anyone in two years. Maybe it's time to jump back into the pool."

"Or maybe I'll never swim again."

"No, but you could try putting your foot in the water to see how it feels."

"If I did that, a gator would come along and chomp my toes off."

Cooper laughed. "Okay, okay. I get it. Listen, the

reason I'm calling, aside from going over some budgeting issues with you, is that Lauren would really like to see you and your new personnel. How's it working out with her so far?"

"Bella is very talented and having them here hasn't been a problem. I hardly see them, except in the kitchen during mealtime."

"That's good news. Marie seems to be lighter on her feet these days, too. She really needed the break. It's a win-win."

"Yep, took me almost dying to figure that conundrum out."

"Don't joke about that. Your accident shaved years off my life."

Jared sighed. "I…know. I'm sorry about that. No more jokes, I promise."

"I'd rather you promise you're not going to be reckless with your life. That's the real promise I want from you."

"I'm not reckless, bro. I know my boundaries. And I'm living my life my way." Hell, their father had died at a very young age, his life cut short by illness. It made Jared realize that he needed to live his life fully, do the things he yearned to do and experience life on his own terms, without fear, without regret. Carpe diem had sunk into his skull. Each and every day he was living his life to the fullest. That was why being laid up was wrestling with his patience.

"If you say so." Cooper didn't sound convinced. "Listen, can we invite ourselves over on Friday night, if you're up to company?"

"Sure thing. Come for dinner and you can taste Bella's cooking."

"Sounds good, thanks. Now, are you up for a talk about next year's budget for the ranch?"

"Yeah, I will be as soon as I get over to the computer."

"Why don't you call me back when you're ready?"

"I'm slow, Coop. Not totally useless. Hang on. It'll just take me a minute."

"Sure. I'm glad to see you're back to being a pain in the ass. Means you're feeling a lot better."

"Funny, Coop. Real funny."

Bella's eyes popped open and she glanced at the digital clock on the nightstand. Yep, 2:00 a.m. She'd gone to bed at ten and four hours was all the sleep goddesses allowed her these days. While her insomnia could be her downfall, she decided long ago that rather than lie in bed and toss and turn for hours, she would get up and do the thing she loved.

The baby slept beside her, all nice and snuggled up tight under the covers, her little head resting on a pillow. Bella bent down and blew an air kiss over her forehead. *Sweet girl*, she mouthed softly before gently sliding off the bed. She checked the video camera set on Sienna—the most valuable invention for a busy mom—and then donned a loose-fitting shift. Tiptoeing out of the room, holding the video monitor, she made her way down the stairs and into the kitchen.

Turning on the light, she set the video monitor on the counter and gave it a glance. Thankfully, Sienna was sound asleep, looking extremely peaceful. Bella sighed and began taking items out of the fridge and cabinets. She had an idea for a wonderful low-cal pizza, but it needed a bit of testing first.

She grabbed a head of cauliflower and quartered it using the chef knife from her new set she was still embarrassed about accepting. Next, she began grating a chunk of cauliflower against a stainless-steel box grater, and tiny pieces of the veggie showered down, covering the cutting board like fallen snow.

Just as she was picking up her second quartered piece, Jared walked in, his eyes blinking against the kitchen lights. He wore a pair of jeans. Period. They hugged his waist below the naval and showed off a washboard chest. Bruises caught her eye for a second, but the beauty of his physique wasn't lost on her, either.

He padded farther into the kitchen. "Hi," he mumbled, sleepy-eyed.

"Gosh, I hope I didn't wake you, Jared."

"That would mean I was sleeping." His mouth crooked up in a smile.

"You weren't?"

"No. I, uh… No. I toss and turn some nights. I figured I'd get up and get something to eat."

"Are you hungry at this hour?"

"A little."

"What can I get you?" She dropped what she was doing and came around the kitchen island.

Jared glanced at her shorty-short shift and then at her legs and suddenly she felt self-conscious. Especially when she could hardly keep her focus on his face while he was standing there bare-chested, his hair mussed, looking quite appealing in a devilish sort of way.

"Nothing. I'll just grab some bread and make a sandwich."

"I'll get it for you," she said, brushing by him.

He gently clamped a hand around her wrist and pulled her back a bit. She turned to find Jared's eyes on her, felt the warmth of his hand covering hers. "You're off the clock, Bella. You don't need to wait on me day and night."

His eyes were soft, his voice tender. And suddenly she was fully aware of Jared Stone, a sensation sweeping through her so raw, so impossibly alluring, that she lost her voice for a second.

He bent his head a little to get her full attention. Little did he know he already had it.

"Okay?"

She swallowed and nodded.

"So, what are you doing here?" he asked, letting go of her hand.

"I hope you don't mind," she said. "I have trouble sleeping, so I use this time to come down and test out some recipes. Don't worry, I eat my mistakes. So there's no food going to waste."

He smiled and sat on a stool at the counter. "Go on with what you're doing. Since I can't sleep anyway, do you mind if I watch?"

"Oh, uh, sure." She couldn't kick him out of his own kitchen. Not that she wanted to, but she wasn't about to analyze why that was. "I can't imagine it's all that interesting, but I don't mind."

She went back to her workstation and glanced at the video monitor. Sienna rolled over, but was still fast asleep.

Jared caught her eye and raised his brows in question.

"I keep an eye on Sienna while she's sleeping. This way if she wakes up, I'll know about it immediately. Lucky for me, she usually sleeps through the night."

"I imagine that monitor is pretty darn handy."

"It is. I'm sure a worried mom invented it."

He laughed. "Probably. So what are you experimenting with?"

"Cauliflower-crust pizza."

Jared made a face. "What?"

"Yes, cauliflower. It's the new kale."

He shook his head.

"It's very healthy for you, low in calories and...well, has many uses. Do you like cauliflower?"

He shrugged. "I suppose, but it's not one of my favorites."

"Well then, you're a good one to experiment on."

"Maybe I should go back to bed." But then he winked and smiled, and Bella relaxed as he leaned his arms on the counter to watch her. Keeping her eyes down on her task, she pretended not to notice his biceps, broad shoulders and muscled chest, but she was aware. Oh, boy, was she aware.

She finished grating the cauliflower and then poured it into the food processor, tossing in minced garlic, oregano and basil. She pulsed it for a few seconds, added one egg and decided to also add in a few tablespoons of almond flour she'd found in the pantry. A few more seconds of pulsing to bind it all together and she hoped she'd have a delicious beginning to her low-cal pizza.

She was beginning to roll out the dough when Jared got up and left the room. She looked up just in time to find Jared walking back into the room, gently pushing his arms into the sleeves of his shirt. His expression faltered but he managed it all on his own.

"You're doing better," she stated while writing down her recipe in her binder.

"A little bit each day, but yeah."

"I'm glad," she said, feeling his gaze on her.

"So what do you put on this pizza exactly?" he asked.

"Anything you like. Why don't you look in the fridge and bring me some things you'd like on the pizza. I've got mozzarella here."

She tipped the dough out onto the surface and began kneading it, over and over. Something swelled within her as she maneuvered the dough, making it flat and round and then patting it down. It was a thing. Maybe a chef thing, or maybe just her thing, but she loved getting her hands into the food, the way gardeners loved digging into the soil.

Jared poked his head inside the fridge. "Doughnuts?"

She made a face. "Eww, Jared."

"How about pickles?"

"I think not."

"Chocolate chips?"

"That could prove interesting," she said, crisscrossing the dough with a rolling pin. "But no for tonight."

"I give up," Jared said.

"Open the crisper. What do you see?"

He slid open the drawer. "Red and green bell peppers, string beans, tomatoes, onions, mango slices and three different kinds of lettuce."

Mango slices? "Pick three of those things." *And don't let one of them be mango.*

Jared carried over onions, tomatoes and red bell peppers.

"That's good for a start," she said. She left the workstation and walked into a double-wide pantry. "Let's see," she said, taking a quick tour of ingredients that might work. "Do you like olives?"

"Love them."

"And, oh, here, how about artichoke hearts?"

"Yep."

"Great, we have our toppings now."

"How about I put on a pot of coffee?" Jared walked over to the coffee machine. "We can have a cup while the pizza is cooking."

She blinked. She hadn't intended for them to eat the pizza now. But he had said he was hungry. "Uh, sure. I'll just chop up some of these veggies and then put the pizza in the oven. I hope it turns out okay."

"Me, too," he said. And then smiled again.

He was messing with her. He had been since he'd walked in here, but she refused to make anything of it. So what if he was charming, he was also her boss at the moment. And business and pleasure mixed like oil and water, to use a foodie phrase.

The coffee brewed as she cleaned the kitchen. Once it was done, Jared poured a cup for both of them and they sat facing each other across the granite-topped island.

The coffee warmed her up and went down deliciously. "Mmm, this is perfect."

"Yep. It's not too bad. Just about the extent of my talent in the kitchen."

"I bet that's not true."

"Oh, wait, I have been known to fry an egg or two."

"Really? How did you ever get by?" *And get to be such a glorious picture of a man.*

"My mama was a good cook. She fed me real good. And then came Marie. I never had to learn."

"Do you want to?"

He put his cup down and leaned forward, the twinkle in his eyes as blue as a sun-drenched lake. "You offering to teach me?"

She tilted her head. Was he flirting? She'd always loved dishing it up with other foodies, but was he serious? "Don't you already have a job?"

He grinned and her heart nearly stopped. "I do. But as you can see, I'm not exactly running to the office every day." He cleared his throat. "I mean my Dallas office."

She couldn't afford to return his flirting. She was out of practice, so much so that she wasn't even sure he *was* flirting. Besides, she had a gigantic wall surrounding her heart stamped with a No Trespassing sign. There was no room behind that wall for anyone other than Sienna.

Certainly not a man like Jared Stone.

Goodness, she still loved Paul. Her heart broke every day from missing him.

"Well, uh…"

"I was just kiddin'," he said. "You've got enough to do around here."

How awkward. She really didn't have a comeback for him. She was busy, but spending more time with a lonely, injured Jared Stone wouldn't be wise.

Because she liked him. It killed her to admit it.

Her nerves jumpy, she sipped her coffee and checked the monitor screen. Anything to avoid eye contact with him.

"How's she doing?" he asked.

"Sawing logs."

"So do you usually stay up the rest of the night?"

"Lord, no. I'll go back to bed in a little while. I might catch another hour or two, maybe three if I'm really lucky and Sienna doesn't wake up. What about you? You said you toss and turn. Is it because you're uncomfortable?"

He gazed at her from just above his mug of coffee and shook his head. "Not tonight."

"Oh, no?" She bit her lip. "So then I did wake you."

"You didn't. Honest. It's just that I'm having…"

"Nightmares?"

He shook his head. "Flashes of memory. I see my car sliding off the road and me losing control. I must've hit some loose gravel and spun out. That's all I remember." He shrugged and stared into her eyes. "It's weird, not knowing what happened. But it's even stranger to see it happen in my mind in sort of slow motion."

"Oh, Jared. I'm sorry."

"Don't be. I'm taking it as a good sign."

"But maybe with the trauma of it all, it's better not to remember."

"Maybe. But whatever happens, I'll deal with it."

He put his hand to his chest and rubbed at his sore ribs. Her gaze fell to that spot and when their eyes finally met, something warm and crazy stirred in her belly.

Immediately she put her head down and stared into her mug.

"What's wrong?"

She shook her head. "Nothing."

"Bella?"

"It's just that I'm feeling guilty." About betraying Paul with her thoughts, her lies to Jared about her true identity and something else entirely.

"What are you feeling guilty about?"

"I might've been the one who broke your ribs."

A speck of acknowledgment flashed in his eyes. "Oh, that."

"You know?"

"I was informed at the hospital that it could've happened when you applied chest compressions."

"If it wasn't for me, you wouldn't be in so much pain."

"If it wasn't for you, I wouldn't be breathing. Besides, there's every possibility the rib injuries were caused by the crash. Let's leave it at that. You shouldn't feel guilty about anything. My ribs will heal. So enough, Bella, okay? No more guilt about anything."

She glanced at his rib cage again, her heart fluttering wildly, and then met his eyes. "Okay."

The timer dinged and she rose instantly, grateful for the distraction. Pulling the pizza out, she was impressed with the results.

"How does it look?" he asked.

She showed him their sizzling veggie-topped creation. "Presentation is important, but what really matters is how it tastes."

"Well, dish it up. I'm dying to try it."

"Me, too."

She used a pizza cutter to slice it and soon they were digging into hot, crusty pieces.

Jared gobbled the first one up. "Oh, wow. It's pretty damn good."

"You really think so?"

"Don't you?" he asked.

She took another bite and chewed, aware of his eyes on her. "I, um, yeah. I think it needs a bit more salt, but it's pretty good. What do you think of the crust?"

"Delicious," he said, grabbing another slice. "You should add it to that cookbook you're going to write."

"I'm writing a cookbook?"

"You *should* write one."

She smiled. "Thank you."

"You made the pizza. I should be thanking you."

"I mean, because...well, it's nice to have someone to experiment on." Someone to encourage her.

"Hey, I'm adventurous, remember. Experiment away."

"As long as you're honest with me, I plan to."

"Yeah, Bella. I promise to always be honest with you. Honesty is something I value above all else."

Bella kept a smile in place but Jared's words seared into her.

And once again guilt replaced her sense of accomplishment over the meal. This time she was demanding something of Jared that she wasn't willing to give herself.

She couldn't be honest with him.

Keeping her secret safe had to be her first priority.

Sienna's future was at stake.

Five

On Friday evening, while Bella put the finishing touches on the meal she was creating for Cooper and his wife, Marie pushed Sienna around the kitchen on her tricycle. "Here we go again, Sienna," Marie said. "You're a good driver."

"I good, Mommy," her daughter parroted.

"Yes, you are, my baby."

"She's getting the hang of this thing." Marie had a note of pride in her voice.

"Goodness, thank you so much, Marie. I just need a few more minutes and I'll be through. Thanks for playing with Sienna for me."

"Nonsense. Anytime," she said, waving her hand in the air. "This little one is the bright spot in my day. I can stay a few more minutes."

Sienna climbed down from her trike and whipped her helmet off, marching over to the big bag of blocks sitting on the floor by the table. "Play bocks?"

Bella rolled her eyes. Sienna had a short attention span. Not that it was unusual for a child her age, but she didn't want to tax Marie overly much. She'd already spent the day doing light housework.

"I sure will, but how about we play them up here on the table?"

Marie hoisted the blocks up and then lifted Sienna onto her lap. The older woman seemed comfortable around children and Bella appreciated her kind nature.

"Thanks," she said again, but Marie was too engrossed in playing with the baby to comment.

Fifteen minutes later, with the dinner cooking and Marie gone, Bella stared at the clothes hanging in her bedroom closet. She didn't think it was fitting to wear jeans with Cooper and his wife coming over, but she didn't really want to dress up, either. Though Jared had made it clear she and Sienna would dine with them tonight, she was still the help. But he'd said Lauren was eager to meet the woman who'd saved his life. Being pregnant, his sister-in-law had been drilling everyone with children about pregnancy and labor and child-rearing and well, Jared seemed to think the world of his sister-in-law. Bella really couldn't argue. She remembered how nervous she'd been about motherhood, too, and she was happy to share her experiences.

She picked out a pair of black slacks and a white scoop-necked blouse with sleeves that billowed out at the wrist. It wasn't fancy, but it wasn't casual, either, and it made her feel soft and female. "How about this one?" she asked Sienna, who was busy crawling around on the floor. "What do you think?"

The baby glanced up at her.

"I'll take that as a yes. Now for you, Sienna-poo." Tonight she wanted to show off her daughter to Cooper and his wife, so she picked out a jumper dress, the top made of light blue denim, the skirt a frilly flare of white voile decorated with bursts of gold.

Bella kept her hair down, wearing it straight. For Sienna, she found an elastic wraparound headband with a big blue bow. She dressed the baby first and then quickly donned her outfit. She was all set to go downstairs and check on dinner when her cell phone chimed.

She smiled when she looked at the screen and answered. "Amy! Hi. How are you?"

"I'm doing just fine. Missing you guys. How's our little girl?"

"Enjoying ranch living, I think. She's being treated very well here. Jared and Marie have been very welcoming. So far, I've managed to keep her happy. If all goes well, tomorrow I plan to take Sienna out to look at the horses. But, oh, we really do miss you. When are you coming to visit? I have Sundays and Mondays off."

"I'll come soon. I promise."

"I'm gonna hold you to that."

"Listen, Bella, I have something to tell you…it may be nothing at all but—"

"Amy, I hate to cut you off," she said, glancing at the digital clock on the nightstand. "Can you tell me later tonight? I'm about to serve dinner and I don't want to burn my first meal for Jared's family."

"Uh, sure. If you're in a rush. Just be sure to call me tonight."

"Amy, is everything okay?"

"Yeah…probably."

"I don't like the sound of your voice. Should I be worried?"

"Bella, I'll tell you later." Her voice brightened. "You go and wow the family with your cooking."

"All right, I'll call you."

Amy had her curious and a bit concerned. But she couldn't dwell on it. She had enough to worry about right now.

She hung up, putting Amy's ominous call out of her mind, and then scooped the baby up. "Here we go. I want you to be a good girl tonight at dinner, okay?"

Sienna laid her head down on her shoulder. "O-tay, Mommy."

Bella beamed inside. For all the bad things that had happened to her in the past, having these sweet moments of absolute joy helped heal her grieving heart. She cherished her baby and would do anything to protect her.

Jared was dressed in a tan snap-down shirt and a new pair of jeans. He'd lost weight since the accident and had ordered new clothes online, but had been a bit skeptical about the whole thing. And damn if the clothes didn't fit him well. He was as groomed as he could manage, a close shave being the least of his worries. He'd done his best trimming his beard.

On his way to the kitchen, the sound of giggles coming from the second floor stopped him cold. He stood at the base of the staircase looking to the top. Bella held Sienna in her arms as they were about to descend. Bella looked beautiful. Correction, she was beautiful, and he might as well stop denying it. His savior, his angel, the woman who'd started his heart on that dark road that night was *stopping* his heart right now. He inhaled deeply and his ribs rebelled.

Damn.

"Hi, Tared." Sienna waved and he was struck again by the vision of the two of them coming down the stairs.

"Hey there, Sienna. Don't you look pretty tonight."

"I pretty?"

"You are," Bella said. "I have to agree with Jared."

As Bella reached the bottom of the stairs, he took a step back. "Hi."

"Hi."

Bella's olive complexion and flowing dark hair made her soft green eyes stand out even more. He couldn't stop staring.

"I, uh…" she said, "I have everything under control. Dinner should be ready in thirty minutes."

"Great. You look nice, too."

"Thank you. I wasn't sure how to dress. I mean, I…"

"We're not formal here, Bella. Anything would've been perfect on you."

Jared blinked. Geesh, did he just say that?

She moved away from him. Like she was scared, or

worse. Maybe she was feeling the same attraction that he was. "I'll go in and check on dinner."

"Need some help?" he asked.

"Not really." She walked past him, heading for the kitchen. "But thanks for the offer."

The doorbell chimed and Jared moved slowly to the door to greet Lauren and Cooper.

Once inside, Lauren gave him a big but gentle hug. "You look really good, Jared. How're you doing?"

"Hanging in. Every day I get a little better. My ribs hurt, but that's gonna take time to heal."

Cooper shook his hand. "Hey, bro. Good seeing you." He put his nose in the air. "Wow, smells really good in here."

"Bella's cooking." Pride registered in Jared's voice and once again he was baffled by the intensity of the feelings he shouldn't be having.

"Where is she?" Lauren said. "I'm dying to meet her."

"She's putting the finishing touches on the meal."

Jared led the way into the kitchen. He made the introductions and Lauren walked directly over to Bella and took her hand. "I'm so sorry about…you know. I apologize for my little indiscretion. Do you think you can forgive me?"

Bella blinked. Lauren wasn't usually so abrupt, but this had obviously been weighing on her.

"I was sort of stunned by it," Bella said earnestly. "But your husband explained your reasons and…well, I do understand why you did it."

"So you forgive me?"

Bella glanced at him and then nodded slowly. "Yes."

"Thank you," Lauren said breathlessly. "I appreciate it so much." She turned to Sienna, who was on a quilt on the floor, deconstructing her block house. Lauren bent down. "Hello, Sienna. My name is Lauren. What do you have here?"

"Bocks."

"Aren't they pretty? I like the purple ones. Which one is your favorite?"

Sienna grabbed one. "Dis one."

"That's a great choice."

Lauren turned to Bella. "She's every bit as cute as Jared said she was."

Bella smiled. "Thanks. Congratulations on your baby. Cooper told me you were expecting."

"Yes, we're excited. And nervous and scared and every emotion under the sun."

"Yeah, I remember that overwhelming feeling. It does get better. How far along are you?"

"Four months. I have a tiny baby bump." She put her hand on her belly.

"Enjoy that tiny feeling while you can."

Lauren laughed. "You're not the first woman to tell me that."

"Don't get me wrong, I loved being pregnant. Just knowing that Sienna was thriving and growing inside me was enough. It's miraculous."

"I agree."

Lauren glanced around the kitchen. "Is there anything I can do to help you out in here?"

"I think I'm good right now. But if Sienna acts up,

I might ask you to entertain her until I get the dinner on the table."

"I'd love to."

"Thanks."

"I've put a dish of appetizers on the dining room table. You all can give them a try and let me know how you like them."

"Sounds good to me," Lauren said. "I'm always famished these days."

"Give a holler if you need anything, Bella," Jared said. "You know where to find us."

Jared led his family to the dining room. Lauren took a seat and then popped a stuffed cherry tomato into her mouth. "She's darling."

Jared grinned. "Sienna's a cute kid."

"I was talking about Bella. And don't pretend you didn't know who I meant."

"Uh, oh, bro. Lauren's got that look in her eye." Cooper sat and grabbed a mini veggie frittata.

"What look?" Jared asked.

"The matchmaking kind," Cooper answered.

Lauren downed another appetizer. "Mmm, these are delish. And I'm not matchmaking. But what do you know about her? Is she dating? Does she have someone in her life?"

Jared shrugged. "Hell, I don't know. I don't talk to her about personal stuff like that. But she's never mentioned anyone. She's got her hands full right now with working and raising a child on her own."

"She's beautiful," Lauren said softly.

"I've noticed…"

Lauren grinned. "I was talking about Sienna this time."

Jared rolled his eyes. His sister-in-law was messing with his head.

"But now that you mention it," she added, "you haven't met anyone quite so nice in a long while."

"I didn't mention it."

Cooper chimed in. "Johnna's been dropping by."

"Coop, please... I'm not interested in Johnna. I'm not interested in anyone."

Lauren covered his hand with hers. Now he was in deep trouble. "It's just that you're a great guy, Jared. You deserve to be happy."

"I am happy. Or I will be as soon as I get the okay to drive again."

Coop sighed. "You can barely walk."

Jared glared at his brother. "I'm walking just fine."

"You know what I think?" Lauren squeezed his hand. "I think that Bella may have been sent here, especially for you. Maybe your angel's not through saving your life."

"It sure was a blessing you were driving down that road that night," Cooper said after forking a piece of chicken into his mouth. "Where were you coming from, Bella? I don't think I've ever asked."

Bella dabbed at Sienna's mouth. The baby sat beside her in the dining room on a makeshift booster chair she'd concocted from a square pillow covered with a towel. The juice from the chipotle peach dressing was dripping down the baby's chin. Her peach chicken dish was messy, but also very delicious. All three of the

Stones had already praised the meal. "My friend Amy and I had taken Sienna to the Winter Wonderland festival off Highway 12. We stopped for a late dinner and Sienna had fallen asleep as soon as she got into the car."

"Your lucky day," Lauren said to Jared.

"I'm not disagreeing," he replied, darting a glance at Bella, the gratitude in his eyes making her a bit uncomfortable. Or was it the heat she saw there that flustered her so much?

"How did Sienna like the festival?" Lauren asked. "She's what? Two years old?"

"A bit younger. She's twenty-two months and I think she liked all the colors and seeing Santa's reindeers. She kept calling them horsies."

"We'll have to remedy that," Jared said. "Tomorrow, I'll show her the stables. She can see our string of horses."

Bella blinked and bit her lip.

"Are you up for that?" Cooper blurted.

Jared's lips twisted and blood rushed to his face. Bella was glad she hadn't said anything. You'd think by the look on Jared's face his brother had emasculated him with that question. Clearly, Jared didn't like limitations of any sort.

"Hey, before you two get into a pissing match— Whoops, sorry, Sienna," Lauren said, turning an apologetic eye to Bella.

She nodded. "It's okay, she didn't hear you."

Lauren went on, "Before you two go at each other, remember that walking is a good form of exercise and if Jared is feeling up to it, he should do it."

"Thank you, Nurse Lauren," Jared said, giving his brother the stink-eye. "I'm feeling much better every day."

"Glad to hear it," Cooper said.

"Your brother is concerned about you, Jared." Lauren spoke in a conciliatory tone. "You're his baby brother. So will you cut him some slack please…for me?"

Jared looked at Lauren and relented. "Yeah, I guess so. I'm just anxious to get back to my life."

"You will, in time. The Stone men aren't known to be patient," Lauren said to Bella. "But they are smart."

"Got that right," Cooper and Jared said in unison.

Everyone laughed and that was that. Immediately the tension in the room disappeared.

"So then, Jared, I suppose we're still on for our annual Christmas party. It's a week away and coming up fast. We didn't want to bring it up until we were sure of your recovery. We can host it this year."

Jared blinked as if he'd forgotten all about Christmas. A few seconds passed, Jared deep in thought. "No, I'll host it," he said unequivocally. "It's my turn."

"Are you sure? We don't mind," Lauren said and then turned to Bella. "The Stones always throw a holiday party for their crew. Family and close friends are invited, too."

"Yes, I'm sure," Jared replied. "You're pregnant and don't need the added work. I'll have the house ready, don't worry."

"That means a tree, and ornaments and decorations, not to mention food," Cooper said.

Jared eyed his brother. "I got it covered."

"I'll help, too," Bella chimed in. "Of course. I'd love to help with the party."

"That's very kind of you, Bella," Lauren said. "We'll all pitch in this year."

"Fine," Jared said grudgingly, looking like he'd rather tangle with a ferocious tiger than plan a holiday party.

"Well, if you're all finished with the meal, I'll get these dishes out of the way." Bella rose.

"Let me help," Lauren said.

"Oh, uh, Lauren, I was hoping you could entertain Sienna for a few minutes while I clean up and serve the dessert. That would be the biggest help. I keep a box of toys for her in the family room."

"If you're sure, I'd love to."

"I'll help Bella," Jared said and this time no one dared question him. "You and Cooper have fun with Sienna. She loves playing with her dolls. And jumping on the sofa. But that's off-limits. It's too dangerous."

Suddenly, Jared was an expert on Sienna? It was strange that she didn't mind the thought. Not at all.

After she got Sienna situated with Cooper and Lauren, she headed back to the dining room. Jared had already cleared the plates from the table. She only had to pick up the glasses and utensils. She met him inside the kitchen. "Thanks for helping."

"Anytime," he said.

"I like your family." She began rinsing off the dishes and arranging them in the dishwasher.

Jared leaned against the counter, next to her. "Even Cooper?"

"Especially Cooper."

"Why?" Jared's sincerely puzzled expression almost made her laugh.

"Because—" she turned to him, meeting his eyes "—he cares so much about you."

Jared's gaze softened and dipped to her mouth. "You're sweet to say that," he whispered.

She was locked in on him, unable to look away, though every bone in her body warned her to step back, to finish her chores and forget about how much she liked this deadly handsome, blue-eyed man standing so close. "You think I'm sweet?"

Jared's lips twitched. "And talented and smart and so beautiful I can hardly pretend not to notice."

"Jared." Was she warning him away or simply sighing his name? She was dizzy from his nearness and unable to figure any of this out.

"Bella, you're my angel." He touched a strand of her hair then, the gleam in his eyes filled with admiration and maybe something more.

"I'm no angel," she whispered.

"To me, you are." He bent his head and she froze.

But Jared's kiss landed on her cheek. "Thanks for a wonderful meal," he said quietly, smiling and then exiting the room.

Disappointed, she touched the spot where he'd just kissed her. She'd been telling herself all along she wasn't attracted to him. She couldn't be. So then why on earth was the skin on her cheek flaming so hot right now?

And why was her heart cracking open a bit when she'd believed it was locked good and tight forever?

* * *

Later that night, after getting Sienna down to sleep, Bella walked into the second bedroom to call Amy back, and her friend picked up right away.

"Hi, Amy."

"Hi. How'd it go over there tonight?"

"It went really well. Jared's got a nice family. Dinner for Cooper and his wife turned out pretty great, but I'm beat and—"

"Sorry to interrupt, Bella. I have something to tell you. I hope it doesn't ruin your sleep."

"What sleep? I don't usually indulge. So what's up?"

"Today the car valet at my condo building said some guy approached him with a picture of you. I got Travis his job at the parking garage, so out of loyalty he didn't say a word, even though the guy offered him a hefty bribe for any information regarding your whereabouts."

"Oh, no." Bella's heart pounded hard.

"Yeah, I know. Crazy, isn't it? Travis is going to get a nice bonus from me, that's for sure. But there's more. Your father has been personally calling my office. He's left a few messages today and I finally had the receptionist tell him I'm out of town. I don't know how long I can get away with that. But even if he finds me, I'll play dumb. He has no idea that we've been in touch. But I'll say one thing—it's a blessing that you're way out there on the ranch, Bella. It's probably the last place your father would ever look for you."

"I hope so." But she wasn't entirely convinced. Her father didn't give up on something when he wanted it badly enough. And now she felt the walls closing in on her. She didn't know if she should leave town or stay put for a while to see if things died down.

She bit her lip hard to keep tears from falling. Except for baby Sienna and her best friend Amy, she didn't trust a soul in the world, and that was a very lonely place to be. "Thanks for letting me know."

"Oh, Bella. You're upset. I'm sorry, honey."

"No, I'm glad you told me. I'll have to be very careful from now on."

"Honestly, I think it's going to be okay. There's no way he can trace you to Stone Ridge Ranch. And I'm certainly not going to tell him what I know. But just to be extra careful, I don't think I should visit you. We probably shouldn't see each other for a while."

"No, probably not." Her heart plummeted. She'd been looking forward to seeing her best friend soon, but Sienna had to come first. Bella had to be beyond cautious now. "I'm bummed about that."

"Me, too."

"Amy, thanks for everything. I don't know what I would do without you. You're the best friend a girl could have."

"Ditto to you, Bella. We'll talk soon. Now, try to get some sleep, okay?"

"Okay."

"'Bye for now."

Three hours later Bella was downstairs in the kitchen. She'd fallen into an exhausted sleep and now she was wide-awake and jittery, Amy's call a few hours ago having thrown her into a tizzy. The best way to remedy her anxiety was to dive right into work. When she was cooking and planning out new recipes, she'd get caught up in the moment and forget her troubles.

From the refrigerator, she grabbed a big loaf of sourdough bread, two cheeses, a slab of bacon, a slice of thick ham and a carton of eggs. She was grateful Marie had stocked up on the groceries she'd requested the other day. She had plenty to work with now.

She buttered a casserole dish and then, wielding her new chef's knife, began cutting off the crust on six slices of bread. At the sound of footsteps approaching, she lifted her head, and her stomach did a little flip as Jared walked into the kitchen. He was rubbing his head, making chunks of his blond hair stick up at odd angles. His mussed, drowsy-eyed look did a number on her already raw nerves.

"Hey," he said quietly. "Didn't think you'd be up tonight. You seemed pretty tired after dinner last night."

After she'd served dessert and said goodbye to Cooper and Lauren, she'd dashed upstairs with Sienna. That kiss, though chaste, combined with Jared's compliments, had ignited something in her that could spell trouble. And she had more than enough trouble right now.

"I was. But my body clock said it was time to get up and so here I am. How about you?"

"Same old. Can't seem to get comfortable in bed." He glanced at her workstation. "What are you making tonight?"

"Your breakfast."

"Really? What is it?"

"Kind of a cheesy egg soufflé. It's really rich, but I'm trying to cut down on the fat content."

"With bacon and ham? Sounds like my kind of dish."

"Hold on, buster, I'm not putting *all* of this into the dish. Bacon and ham will be added for flavor. And I'm going to cut the eggs down to three whites and three whole eggs."

"Okay, so burst my bubble. Want some milk?" he asked, heading to the refrigerator.

She shook her head. "No, but please leave it out. I need some for the recipe."

Jared poured himself a tall glass of milk and then took a seat across from her at the workstation to watch her. It was getting to be a thing, these after-midnight meetings.

He sat quietly for a while, sipping his drink. She was fully aware of his eyes on her. "Am I disturbing your quiet?" he asked.

As in, was his presence here making her nervous? Heck yes. But she didn't mind him being here. He was a nice diversion after that disturbing phone call from Amy.

"Actually, if I'm totally honest, I don't mind. Sienna is always interrupting my thoughts and I love her beyond belief, but sometimes it's nice to be able to have a conversation without being disturbed."

"I get that. You can turn off being Mommy for a little while."

"Something like that."

"You know, Cooper and Lauren were impressed with

you," he said. "And Lauren's amazed at how you keep it all together, work and baby and single parenthood."

She kept her eyes on her task. Was she keeping it all together? She was on the run, trying to protect her baby and lying through her teeth to some very decent people about who she really was.

During dessert, she and Lauren had had a long talk about babies and pregnancy, and she'd shared with her a little about her life with Paul. But she'd had to omit so much from that conversation to keep her identity a secret.

"To tell you the truth, you impress me, too," Jared said.

She shrugged. Normally, Jared's compliment would have gone to her head, but tonight she was trying to keep things real. And nothing was more real than learning her father may have sent his henchmen out to find her. "I'm doing what I have to do. Sienna's the most important thing in my life. And as you can see, I can survive on very little sleep, so I have that over other women. I have a few more hours in my day."

"I guess so," he said, polishing off his milk and setting the glass down with a soft thud. "Can I help with anything?"

He was a gorgeous hunk of a man—how could she not notice?—but that wasn't why she was drawn to him. The bond of her saving his life would always be there, but more than anything she truly liked him and enjoyed talking to him. He was easy and nice and...well, she needed a friend so badly right now. "Can you cut up bacon and ham?"

"I can do that."

He came around the granite counter and she handed him a knife. "Just call me your sous chef."

"Do I have to?"

He laughed and it was the first time she'd seen him laugh without visible pain. It soothed her heart to witness him healing. "Yes."

"Okay, if you say so. You're the boss."

"Not in the kitchen, I'm not." Jared smiled. "You're in charge in here. From now on, I'm gonna call you the Midnight Contessa."

Contessa? She actually liked the sound of it. Deliberately, she hadn't made reference to her Italian heritage to Jared, and it was just one more thing she felt guilty about. But the name had a nice ring.

"Feel free to use it as the title of your cookbook."

She could only return half a smile tonight. He had more faith in her than she had in herself. The cookbook and her dream of opening a restaurant had been put on hold indefinitely. She couldn't think that far into the future. She had to take one day at a time right now.

She hoped Jared didn't notice her anxiety. It would only lead to questions that she couldn't answer.

"Maybe someday, Jared."

They worked together, cooking up the diced bacon and ham, lining the casserole dish with bread and then adding the rest of ingredients. When it was all assembled, she put the dish into the oven and set the timer.

"What now?" he asked.

"Now I clean up the kitchen and wait. But you don't have to, if you'd rather try going back to sleep."

"Not on your life. This is my first sous chef creation."

"It'll take at least half an hour."

"Hey, I have an idea. Wait right here."

"I'm not going anywhere," she said, dumbfounded. "I'll just start cleaning."

But Jared was already out of the room. Not three minutes later he came back holding a suede jacket and a plaid wool shirt.

"What's all this?"

"We need some fresh air." He picked up the baby monitor and then grabbed Bella's hand and tugged her to the French door leading out to the large stone patio area. "Here, put this on," he said, handing her the suede jacket.

He left her to fiddle with knobs and buttons on a fire pit and the next thing she knew, she was sitting on a comfy outdoor sofa in front of a blazing fire. Jared sat beside her and warmth surrounded them.

"I haven't come out here in a long while," he said. "I've forgotten how beautiful the stars were. Look at that sky, Bella."

She glanced skyward. "It is quite amazing. So why haven't you come out here? Is it because of your injuries?"

"No, happened way before that. It used to remind me of…never mind."

"What?" she asked softly. "What did it remind you of?" She was really curious. Jared usually didn't speak much about himself and she was eager to learn more about him.

"Just a girl I once…cared for."

"Oh, so you would come out here with her?"

"Yeah, and we'd talk for hours about our future."

"I take it it didn't work out."

"No, it didn't."

"I'm sorry, Jared."

He took his eyes off the stars to glance at her. "I'm over it. Just kicking myself for being stupid."

"I doubt you were ever stupid."

He scratched his head. "No, I was. I trusted her, believed in her, even when I should've been more wary. Things weren't adding up and I was too damn blind to see it. She lied to me over and over, and it was her betrayal that really did a number on me."

Bella shivered. She could put herself into that equation and the results would be the same. Lies and betrayal and abuse of his trust.

"Hey, you're trembling." Jared rose and sifted through a patio box, coming up with a soft gray woolen blanket. He sat beside her and tucked her into the blanket. "Sorry, didn't realize you were cold."

"I...shouldn't be." Her trembling had nothing to do with the temperature.

"Better now?" he asked, his eyes filled with genuine concern.

"Much."

Satisfied, he leaned back and put his arm around her. Cushioned by his warmth, she gazed at a sky full of twinkling specks of light. She sighed and her guilt about lying to Jared was immediately replaced by a soothing calm. "Thank you for bringing me out here tonight. It's just what I needed."

"Welcome," he said, smiling. He seemed pleased that

he'd pleased her. A girl could let that go to her head. "You seemed a little... I don't know, sad? Or upset. I thought the fresh air and bright stars might brighten your mood."

He'd picked up on her anxiety? Here she'd thought she'd covered it so well.

"I'm...okay, Jared. Some days are more difficult than others."

"I get how hard this is for you. You being a *widow* and all," he said ultra quietly, as if the word would somehow set off a whirlwind of emotion. "And if you ever need anything, I'm here, Bella. All you have to do is ask."

She turned her body slightly, looking him in the eyes. She lifted her hand to his cheek and the fine stubble tickled her fingertips. "Thank you."

She leaned forward and placed a kiss on his cheek. And then he turned toward her and their mouths brushed, a gentle, tender caress that felt as natural as the sun shining. His lips were warm and firm and she waited for guilt to summon her, for a backlash of forbidden emotion to warn her off, but none of that happened. Instead she relished the kiss, savored the taste of him, enjoyed the sweeping sensations her body was experiencing.

She'd been wound tight lately and Jared coming to her rescue tonight soothed her nerves. And now kissing him was...well, putting only wonderful thoughts in her head.

"Bella." He called her name reverently, his tone humble and seemingly surprised. His hand cradled her face as his lips became more demanding. Kissing him was like a balm to her internal wounds, a safe haven where she could forget. "Tell me to stop, Bella. If you don't want this."

"Don't stop," she whispered.

A pent-up groan rose from Jared's throat and he took her into his arms, wrapping her in an embrace. The glow of the fire, the twinkling stars and the fresh bite in the air together gave her a sense of amazing peace and comfort.

She felt safe with Jared. It was as simple as that.

And she ignored all the warnings screaming at her to be careful. To be wise. To be smart.

She'd needed solace and Jared was providing it. Her body was slowly awakening from a yearlong slumber. How good it was to feel alive again.

Jared kissed her deeper now and she accepted him into her mouth. The touch of his tongue on hers changed from sweet sensations to pulse-pounding heat, and she gave in to the yearnings to touch him. She wrapped her arms around his neck and the blanket separating them slipped away, bringing her body up against his.

Her breasts crushed his chest.

"Oh, man, Bella," he muttered. "I wanted to be conscious if you ever brought your mouth to mine again, but this is better than I'd ever imagined."

It amazed her that he'd been imagining kissing her. She sighed into his mouth, the temptation to touch him further, to unsnap his shirt and feel the heat pulsing in his chest was battling with her sense of decorum. So far, they'd only kissed, but if she was bold enough to undress him, it would be an open invitation for him to do the same and she didn't know if she was ready for that.

A buzzing rattled in her ears.

The timer to her soufflé was going off.

They both froze and Jared backed away first. "My breakfast," he said, heat glimmering in his eyes.

"Your breakfast," she repeated, the burn of his lips imprinted on her.

Jared rose first and gave her a hand up. She took it and they faced each other. "Bella, promise me you won't be sorry about any of this."

He stared into her eyes, her answer important to him. "I promise. I won't be."

He nodded and took a gulp of air. "Okay, I'll see you in the morning."

"Good night, Jared."

And as if he meant to hold her to her promise, he bent his head and kissed her once more before opening the door for her to reenter the house.

The next morning she and Sienna strolled hand-in-hand along the path next to Jared. Good on his word, he was taking them to see the horses. "Cooper's got a bigger string of horses at his place, but I kinda like our stable. And we've got a new foal, a filly to show Sienna. I think she's gonna like Pumpkin Pie."

Sienna's ears perked up. "Punkin."

"Yes, baby girl. That's the horse's name," Bella said. "It's a little one, just like you."

Sienna stared up at the tall rancher. "Tared's horsie."

"That's right, Sienna," he said to her, smiling.

Sienna smiled back and reached for Jared's hand, her fingertips touching his knuckles. Jared's blue eyes melted for an instant as he folded her daughter's hand into his. He glanced at Bella, shrugging, an awed expression on his face.

Her instincts were telling her this wasn't a good thing, but she couldn't dismiss seeing the joy in Sienna's eyes as they approached the corral.

"Here we are." Jared stopped at the fence, where half a dozen horses were frolicking around the perimeter of the corral.

"Let's take a better look, Sienna." Bella lifted her daughter up, setting her little boots on the second rung of the fence to give her a better view of the animals.

"Mommy!" Sienna pointed to the filly, the smallest creature in the corral with a reddish-bronze coat.

"That must be Pumpkin."

"It sure is," Jared said. "She's sticking close to her mommy."

Sienna took it all in, fascinated.

"It's a big corral," Bella said. "How many horses do you have here?"

"About a dozen. Make that thirteen," he said, tipping his hat back on his forehead. "If I'm counting the new filly."

"Do they all get along?"

"Seem to. But we build our corrals oval, which keeps the horses from bunching up in corners and getting too territorial. Makes everyone happy."

"If only people were like that," she said, thinking aloud.

Her cryptic comment brought Jared's head up and

he stared at her, his brows raised in question. She swallowed hard, condemning herself for letting down her guard.

"You all right, Bella?"

She looked into his eyes, wishing she could tell him the truth.

As much as she thought things might've gotten weird between them this morning, they hadn't been at all. Jared had been as earnest and forthright as usual and she'd sort of fallen into a sweet ease with him. Slowly her qualms about the kiss they'd shared had disappeared, though it helped that she had Sienna as a buffer.

Bella was still wondering what that kiss had meant to Jared.

For her, it was a gentle release of anxiety, a grasp at something solid and real amid the lies she'd told. It was a way to relieve her fear about her father finding her. But a part of her felt as if she'd been cheating on Paul. She was not all right, but she couldn't tell Jared that.

How had her life become so complicated?

"Sure, I'm good," she said, nodding, doing her best to convince him.

He nodded back. A beautiful black-and-white mare strolled over to the fence and Sienna began flapping her arms. "Horsie! Horsie!"

"I see it."

"Say hello to Jubilee, Sienna," Jared said. "She's just a little older than you. She's a sweetheart, just like you. You want to pet her?"

Before Bella could stop him, Jared lifted Sienna higher and leaned over the fence. Her daredevil daughter didn't protest at all. Jared's hand covered Sienna's as he carefully guided her toward the horse's flank. "There you go, Sienna. How does that feel? You just have to treat her nice."

"Nice," Sienna parroted as she stroked the horse over and over.

"That's it," Jared said. "Maybe one day you'll get to ride one of these sweet girls."

"Not on your life," Bella said, her inner mama bear coming out.

Jared slid her a sideways glance. "Don't worry, Sienna. Your mama will change her mind."

"I don't think so. She's too young."

"I was one when I took my first ride."

"You grew up on a ranch."

"What difference does that make?" he asked.

"I don't know. It doesn't, I guess."

"Where did Sienna grow up anyway?" he asked. "I don't think you've told me."

"Not on a ranch." Bella reached for Sienna, taking her out of Jared's arms, rattled by his question. She didn't want to lie to him. As far as he knew, she'd been living in Dallas.

Jared flinched.

And she felt like an uncaring jerk for being abrupt with him. "Did she hurt your ribs?"

"No, she didn't." Jared thought about that a few seconds. "She didn't hurt my ribs," he repeated, looking stunned by the revelation. Then he grinned, the smile consuming his entire handsome face. Again, a little jolt of joy streamed through her system at Jared's healing.

Each day he was getting stronger. "I can lift this little peanut without any pain."

Bella put her hand on his forearm and squeezed. "That's good."

Jared glanced at her hand on his arm and his eyes shuttered closed as if relishing her touch. She was suddenly self-conscious, her mind instantly flashing back to being in his arms last night, however briefly, and kissing him.

"It's not just good, it's damn near amazing. A few days ago, I was having trouble breathing."

The hopeful gleam in his eyes chipped away at all her internal warnings.

"I'm glad, Jared. That's wonderful news."

"Yeah," he said, ruffling Sienna's dark mop of hair. "It is."

Six

Sienna giggled as Marie wrapped shimmery gold garland around her body all the way up to her neck. And Bella plopped a big red bow on top of her head. "You're just about the cutest Christmas tree I ever did see, little one," Marie said.

They were in the middle of the living room surrounded by Christmas boxes. Garland and lights and snowmen, almost life-size reindeer as well as different variations of Santa Claus filled the room. There was a whole shed full of decorations sitting on the living room floor brought in by some of the Stone Ridge crew.

She and Marie had decided to start in here first, and were both getting a kick out of Sienna's enthusiasm. Not that she knew much about Christmas yet, but she loved being in the middle of the decorations, or rather, being a *part* of the decorations.

"Let's sort these all out and decide what room to put them in," Bella said. "And once Sienna goes down for her nap, we'll be able to decorate."

"That sounds like a fine plan," Marie said. "Maybe Jared will be able to lend a hand, too, that is if he wants to. He's not been keen on the holidays ever since…"

Marie buttoned her lips, but the sentence she'd left hanging stirred Bella's curiosity too much not to ask. "Why doesn't he like the holidays?"

"It's just that…that woman broke his heart right after Thanksgiving. They'd been planning a Christmas wedding."

"Really? I had no idea." She bit her lip, remembering the conversation they'd shared on the patio last night. He'd opened up to her a bit about his love life, but he never mentioned he was to be married.

"He doesn't talk much about it, but ever since then, Jared's been an ole Scrooge about Christmas."

"Like he's going through the motions for family and friends, when he'd rather be anywhere else in the world?"

Marie sent her a thoughtful look. "I think that's exactly it."

Bella could relate. Ever since Paul's death, nothing seemed right. No holiday was the same. And his accident had happened right before Thanksgiving, so she really understood the pain and heartbreak he'd gone through at a time when everything was supposed to be jolly and bright.

"What happened between them?" Bella asked.

Marie shook her head. "It's not for me to say, but I will tell you that woman really deceived him and messed with his emotions."

Bella squeezed her eyes shut briefly. "That's awful." And it was also awful that she'd been lying to Jared since the moment he'd set eyes on her. Bella sat on the parlor sofa, shaken.

"Dear? Are you all right? You just turned pale as a bowlful of oats."

Jared came into the room and glanced around, smiled at silly Sienna and then studied Bella from head to toe. "What's wrong?"

"Nothing," she said, sitting straighter in her seat.

"All of a sudden the color drained from her face," Marie said. "Jared, maybe you should take her outside. I think she needs some fresh air."

"Will do," he said.

"No, don't be silly. I'm…fine."

Marie shook her head adamantly. "You need air, Bella. You two go on. And while you're outside, Jared, please take a look in the shed for the nativity scene. I don't see it here. I'll take Sienna into the kitchen for a snack. Come on, little one," Marie said gently, unraveling the garland surrounding her and taking her hand. "I think I found some animal crackers just for you." Sienna followed Marie out of the room.

Bella stood to face Jared. "This is not necessary."

"Marie says it is and I learned a long time ago not to argue with a force of nature. C'mon, I need your help anyway. The nativity scene is the one decoration that must go up. It's a Stone family tradition."

"Okay, Jared. But only to help you search because there's nothing wrong with me."

Jared grinned and led the way, saying over his shoulder, "I've noticed."

His compliment went straight to her head.

She sighed and exited the house. They walked side by side, Jared commenting on the cooler weather to come. She was used to San Francisco fog and clouds and cold winter nights. It was nothing new to her. But Jared believed she lived in Dallas with Amy, so she wasn't going to say too much. "So what do you do when you're not working with your brother?" she asked.

"I have a few other enterprises and an office in Dallas, which I've been neglecting lately. But I have a good team that's covering for me while I'm out. I tend to get restless just being on the ranch, so I became a novice entrepreneur."

"Must keep you really busy."

"I like the challenge."

"You're not a homebody?"

"Me? No. That would be Coop. He's happy on Stone Ridge."

"And what makes Jared Stone happy?" she asked.

"Let me show you," he said, leading her into a five-car garage attached to the house. It was dark inside until Jared flipped on the overhead lights. Squinting at first, she focused her eyes. They were standing in a showroom of expensive cars and motorcycles. "I guess you could call this my hobby."

"Wow. This is amazing." She turned to face him and smiled. "So, you're in the new car business."

His eyes lit up. "Funny girl."

She smiled again and strolled around the garage, taking in a white Corvette convertible, a jet-black Jaguar, a souped-up Jeep and two motorcycles. One she recognized as a Harley-Davidson. Everything represented speed and danger. That's what made Jared Stone tick.

Jared followed directly behind her and she was keenly aware of his presence. There was something incredibly intimate being in here with him, as if he was revealing his true self to her. As she turned to him, she found pride in his eyes and a boyish eagerness. Her nerves began to tingle.

"It's all really nice," she said, holding back her reservations about the danger these cars represented. Jared was a grown man and she couldn't very well lecture him when she'd married a man who'd flown helicopters for a living, sometimes under extreme conditions. "Do you have a favorite?"

He stood close, very close. "That would be the pile of ashes I left on the road."

"Oh…sorry." But a car could be replaced. Jared had been lucky to walk away from that accident without any permanent damage to his body. The memory of that night still made her queasy. The bond she had with him was growing stronger every day.

"I'm getting over it," he said, taking a strand of her hair in his hand. She swallowed hard, seeing this man so close up under the bright lights and noticing not one flaw on his handsome face. "I wouldn't have met you otherwise."

"Jared," she said on a breath.

"You're my angel, Bella. And I can't stop thinking about kissing you again."

"We shouldn't," she whispered without too much resolve because inside she was melting. Inside, her heart ached for a bit of tenderness to help her forget her terrible grief. Inside, she wanted the comfort and, yes, the excitement of being in Jared's arms once again.

He cupped her face in his hands. "I know you're still hurting, Bella. Tell me to back off and I will. I promise." His reverent tone tugged at her heart. "But I need to hear you say it."

She stared at him and no words formed on her lips. No refusals. She couldn't tell him to back off. She couldn't walk out of there and turn her back on him.

"Bella."

She heard desperate desire in his voice and a vulnerability that washed away her doubts.

His hands wrapped around her waist, his fingers inching her closer. She put up no resistance as he bent his head. The first brush of his firm lips on hers sent her flying and she moved closer to him and wrapped her arms around his neck. He was tall and she stood on tippy toes to reach his mouth more solidly.

His kiss was more demanding than last night, more powerful, and her heart fluttered wildly in her chest now, her body melding to his with less hesitancy. Their tongues did a mating dance amid her moans and his groans. Jared woke her body from its doldrums, making her feel free and alive and vital.

His hands slid underneath her butt, his fingertips pressing into the soft cheeks as he lifted her up and set her gently onto the hood of his Jaguar. Thrills raced through her belly and she became instantly aware of where this could lead as Jared's dizzying kisses kept coming.

He pulled away to stroke a finger down her cheekbone, his eyes blazing blue heat. "Angel," he said and then smiled and kissed her again.

She lay back against the hood of the car, taking him with her. "Jared," she whispered.

That one word gave him permission to take what she offered, and Jared only hesitated for a brief, maybe surprised, moment before he brought his hand to the dip in her blouse. His fingertips scraped the top rim of her breast and shock waves erupted from the sheer pleasure of his touch. If she reacted like this from one touch, she could only imagine what making love to him would be like. Suddenly, awfully, she wasn't as opposed to that notion as she should be.

He was unbuttoning the first button on her blouse when his phone buzzed.

Their eyes met.

"I don't have to get that," he said, sighing.

"You do. It could be about Sienna."

He squeezed his eyes closed briefly, acknowledging that fact. He moved away to reach into his pocket and pull out his phone. "Yeah, hi, Marie."

Bella sat up and then jumped down from the Jaguar's

hood, her heart racing for another reason now. She listened to Jared's conversation.

"Yeah, you're probably right. Okay, I'll go get it from Coop's house."

"Ask her how Sienna is," Bella chimed in.

"How's Sienna?"

Jared listened and nodded. "Okay, I'll tell Bella. No problem. Thanks."

She waited patiently for Jared to hang up. "What?"

"Sienna's fine. She actually conked out after her snack and Marie put her down for a nap. She's staying with her."

"Okay, good. Jared listen…uh, about—"

He folded her into his arms. "Shush," he said, kissing the top of her forehead. And she felt so safe, so cherished, in his arms, she didn't say the silly platitudes she was going to say about not knowing her own heart, about not reading too much into this, about how this wasn't a good idea. Honestly, right now she didn't know if she truly believed any of it anyway.

"Marie remembered that the nativity scene is at Coop's house," Jared said softly. "Come with me to pick it up?"

"I don't know. Sienna—"

"Is sleeping. Marie's watching her and it's only gonna take twenty minutes. I promise."

Bella blinked, debating. Jared grabbed her hand and tugged her toward his Corvette. "C'mon, Bella. I want to take my first ride with you by my side."

"You can't drive, Jared." She pulled him to an abrupt

stop, hardly realizing her own strength. "Tell me you didn't mean that."

"I'm not going to drive. You are."

She blinked, catching his meaning after a second or two. "I certainly am not!"

"Why not?"

"Because…because…"

"See…you can't come up with a reason."

"I don't want to," she said. Wasn't that reason enough?

"Okay…then you leave me no choice. I'm gonna have to get behind the wheel." Jared made a move toward the driver's side of the car.

"Oh, for heaven's sake. Move over," she said, angling her body between him and the car. "I'll drive."

Jared grinned. "That'a girl."

It wasn't as if she hadn't driven a sports car before. She'd been given an Alfa Romeo on her seventeenth birthday. It was a beautiful car, but she'd hated driving it. She wasn't showy or status-conscious and she didn't have a need for speed. The car had been impractical and made no sense for a college student. After a year and some arguing with her father, she'd traded it in for a much more sensible sedan. It was just another way she'd disappointed Marco.

"I'm only doing this to keep you from reinjuring yourself. You haven't gotten permission to drive from your doctor yet, have you?"

"That'll happen soon enough. It's just a formality now." He put out his arms. "I'm fit."

Glancing over his solid body, she couldn't argue that point. "You sure are."

He grinned and opened the Corvette's door for her. "I like you, Bella Reid. A lot."

"Call me crazy, but I like you, too." A lot.

Just minutes later Bella's hair was blowing in the breeze, the car kicking up all kinds of dust behind them. It was a short drive on Stone property to Cooper's place. Gosh, he looked totally at home in this car, and happy. She smiled. She'd kept Jared from driving and breaking all kinds of speed laws.

She, on the other hand, was breaking all sorts of laws of her own making.

And Jared Stone was at the heart of it all.

Jared was definitely sleeping better, his wounds healing and his sore ribs not so restrictive anymore. Yet his internal clock still woke him anyway at precisely half past one. As he lay in bed a couple days later, his first thoughts were of Bella, her soft lips under his, her body meshing against him as he'd kissed her. It was no use pretending he could wish these feelings away. The more time he spent with Bella, the more he wanted her. Kissing her filled all the voids in his body, corking up his heartache over Helene and filling the emptiness in his life.

She was preparing a meal in his kitchen right now and was careful not to make much noise, but he'd heard her come downstairs ten minutes ago because he'd been listening for her. Now he was in bed battling his conscience and warring with the lust he had for her. She was his employee, a woman whose heart had been broken just one year ago. He admired her, liked her, cared for her. She was the whole package of beauty, talent and sweetness all rolled up into one.

Something was happening between them and it was stronger than his willpower to just let it be. It was stronger than his internal warnings not to get involved with her. She was just steps away and it was killing him to hold back, to keep his distance.

Who knew what would've happened the other day if Marie's phone call hadn't interrupted them.

The digital clock flashed. Another minute had gone by. Eleven minutes. Was that all his willpower could afford?

Hell yeah.

He tossed off the covers and rose from bed. Moonlight streamed into his room. He slipped his arms through the sleeves of his shirt, ignoring the slight ache to his ribs, and slid on a pair of jeans. He strode out of the bedroom, padding toward the kitchen, eager to see Bella. He found her hard at work at the counter, surrounded by bowls and equipment and ingredients, jotting down her recipe on a piece of paper.

It made him smile. And suddenly he felt selfish for disturbing her and had a good notion to hightail it out of there. Just as he was about to turn around, she spoke up. "Ready for some milk?"

He glanced at the milk container sitting out next to an empty glass on the counter. Had she been waiting for him? Joy surged in his gut and he wasn't going to second-guess it. "The Midnight Contessa is hard at work again." He walked farther into the kitchen.

"That would be me. Can't sleep?"

"No. Not too much." Technically it wasn't a lie. But he wasn't going to admit he loved these late-night meetings with her.

"Sorry to hear that. But you seem so much better lately," she said, keeping her eyes on the flour and butter she was measuring.

"I'm getting better every day. Nights are harder to relax."

"Speaking from one night owl to another."

He laughed. "I guess. Hey, how about putting me to work, I'm too antsy to just sit here."

"I can do that. Help me get this dough together. Pinch and squeeze the flour to the butter like this," she said. He watched her over his shoulder as he made his way to the sink to wash his hands.

When he approached, she slid over and made room for him at the workstation. He dipped his hands into the large bowl of what would be dough soon and every so often her hand would graze his. Just a simple touch from her swelled his chest and put illicit thoughts in his head. He enjoyed working with her, seeing her make decisions, putting great thought into what she was doing. "I hope this is gonna be blueberry pie."

"Nope, not even close."

"You're not making pie?"

"*We're* not making pie. Sorry to disappoint you, but this is an experiment. I'm attempting to make a meatless pot pie using veggies and tofu."

Tofu? Jared blinked, trying to think of a tactful response. "Good Lord, why?" was all he could come up with. "I mean, hasn't someone already invented it?"

"Yes, but I'm trying to make it better."

Jared shook his head, cautious not to hurt her feelings. "Uh, that explains it." He stood close enough to see her long lashes flutter, her expression becoming thoughtful while their hands brushed against each other in the mixing bowl.

A chuckle rumbled out of her mouth. "You hate the idea."

"Not hate."

"And you're trying to spare my feelings."

"I have simple tastes, Bella. But you've already impressed the hell out of me. With your cooking," he added. And with a whole lot more.

"Really?"

"Really," he said emphatically.

Her shoulders slumped and she sighed. "You're right. I wasn't exactly inspired, and you have to be when you're developing recipes. This is one adventure we won't go on together."

"Bella," he said quietly, "I'd go on any adventure with you." He laced their dough-covered fingers together and brought their hands out of the bowl. Her soft green eyes lifted to his.

"I'll make you blueberry pie, Jared," she whispered.

"Suddenly I have an appetite for something sweeter." His gaze dipped to her mouth as her lips parted and he wasn't about to miss the opportunity to kiss her. He'd been consumed with it since the very first time they'd kissed.

He touched her lips again, taken by her softness, by the tantalizing taste of her. She gasped—a swift inhalation of breath. He hoped he was reading her correctly. Stuck between deep desire and hopeless honor, he couldn't go on without knowing one thing. "Bella," he whispered over her mouth. "I can't seem to stay away from you. Tell me to stop. Tell me and I'll leave you alone. Your job will never be in jeopardy, I promise."

"I know that," she whispered back, relieving his innermost fear. "You're not harassing me, Jared. Just the opposite. When I'm with you, some of the sadness goes away." She cupped his face in her hands and gave him a sweet kiss on the mouth. "I don't know any more than that."

It was enough. Hell, it was everything he'd needed to hear.

She smiled at him. "You've got flour on your face."

"Thanks to you," he said.

"Let me just wipe it away," she said, rising on tiptoes and using her mouth to brush it away with tiny, moist kisses.

The woman was killing him in small doses, but he wasn't complaining. His heart was fuller than he could ever remember. "I like the way you clean."

"Do you?" Her head tilted coyly, all her lush black hair falling out of its clip.

Jared swallowed hard, loving the sight of her in her apron smudged with flour, her hair freely flowing.

He dipped his hand into the flour and touched her

face, marking her, and then began sprinkling flour along her neck and throat and onto the luscious hollow between her breasts. "Looks like you could use a little cleanup, too."

Bella looked down at herself and giggled. The sweet sound brought a grin to his face and he reached for her, his hands circling her waist. He bent her backward in his arms and started his cleanup, licking the deep valley between her breasts. His heart beat like a sensual drum, deeper, harder, and as he kissed her soft, smooth skin over and over, the drumbeat slid lower, pulsing at his groin.

He touched her breasts through the material of her apron and groaned, making his way up her throat, kissing her chin and finally finding promise at her lips.

The little noises erupting from her throat relayed her pleasure and suddenly that was all Jared wanted to do—to give her pleasure. He kissed her again and again until the flour smudges on her body were good and gone and the noises she made became gasps and moans.

She trembled in his arms. "Bella," he whispered in a plea. "I need you."

He'd said *need* and not *want*, and it dawned on him immediately that he did need her, more than he'd ever needed a woman in his life. She was his angel and he'd be a damn fool to screw this up. "God." He stopped kissing her and put his head down, gently bumping his forehead to hers. "Tell me you feel it, too."

Bella didn't hesitate. "I feel it, too. I don't want you to stop, Jared. Maybe I should, but I don't."

"Come to bed with me, angel."

"I'm no angel, Jared," she insisted softly, grabbing the baby monitor and taking his outstretched hand.

"That's not true, sweetheart, but I'm not opposed to you proving me wrong…in the bedroom."

Bella set the baby monitor down on Jared's dresser, her heart beating in her ears. Her first priority always had to be Sienna, and fortunately her baby was sound asleep. Jared glanced at the baby monitor, too, and nodded. A big part of her wanted to believe Jared Stone cared about her and her baby, and not just because she'd saved his life, not just because he wanted a temporary bed partner.

He began unsnapping his shirt and she caught herself watching him as if she was floating in a dream, mesmerized by his elegant, swift motions and partly stunned that she was here in his bedroom in the first place.

Thoughts of Paul strummed in her head and she had no choice but to shove them aside or she'd start running. She couldn't live in the past. She'd been through a lot this year, and if being with Jared would help her get over her heartache, she had to take the chance.

She focused on him. He was nothing short of perfect, even in his slightly bruised state. Moonlight touched his profile and the sharp angles of his jaw looked hard and dangerous, but she knew he wasn't. She knew what kind of man Jared was and that's why she was here with him.

His shirt off now, he reached for her hand and laid it on his bare, muscled chest. She inhaled deeply, her fingertips scorched by his heat. His whole body seemed

on fire and the flames spread to her like wildfire. His
eyes closed as she slid her hand over him again and
again, absorbing his rock-solid feel. It was as if he was
absorbing her touch, as well.

"Jared," she murmured.

He claimed her mouth again and his hands wrapped
around her back to untie her apron and lift it off her.
From there, her shift easily followed as he gave it a tug
at the shoulders. It slid off her body, circling her feet.
She took a step out of it, fully aware that she was standing before Jared almost naked but for the tiny white bra
and panties she wore.

His eyes burned into her as he reached around her
again, this time flicking the fastener of her bra. He
guided the straps down her arms, until she was free
of the garment. Her long hair tickled the tips of her
breasts, covering her from his view. Gently, he moved
her hair aside, grazing her nipples with the back of his
hands. She gasped.

And so did he. "Bella. Your name suits. You're…
beautiful."

His eyes locked to hers, he cupped her breast, gently
weighing and rubbing it with the palm of his hand, his
thumb circling the aroused tip. Ribbons of heat flowed
down her belly and a tiny moan escaped her mouth. He
kissed away her next moan and the next and, before
she knew what was happening, she was lying across
Jared's bed, her head against a fluffy pillow, and he
was over her, his erection pressing her belly through
his denim jeans.

He was thorough in his kisses, making sure she was

satisfied, and then he backed off for a few seconds, adjusting his position. The flat of his hand traveled from her breast down her torso, past her navel. Jared worked her panties down her legs and her heart rate escalated in anticipation.

When his palm finally touched her folds, she parted her legs for him and he stroked her over and over, his fingers working magic on her body. The painful pleasure shocked her and soon jolts of electricity streamed through her body. Her breaths came in short bursts, her hips arched and trembled, and a low unavoidable whimper escaped her mouth. Her release shattered, sending pieces of pleasure to all parts of her body. It was complete and abundant and so freaking amazing.

"Jared… Jared."

"I'm here, angel."

"That was so…"

"I know. I'm glad," he said, giving her a smile right before he kissed her.

She lay naked on the bed, fully exposed to him after having a mind-blowing orgasm, and there was no shame, no guilt, which sort of baffled her. Nothing about this night seemed wrong.

But she knew there should be plenty wrong with this scenario: namely that she was lying to Jared, deceiving him about her true identity. And for Sienna's safety, she couldn't do a thing about it.

His next kiss caused all thoughts and doubts to vanish from her head. She was in Jared territory now, a place she craved to be.

"I've got protection, Bella," he said, rising quickly

to remove his jeans and briefs. She watched him sheath his erection and took a big gulp of air. Good Lord, he was magnificent and, for the night at least, all hers.

"Somehow, I knew you would."

He smiled a killer smile, cocking his head to one side. "You'd be surprised."

"I'm hoping to be."

He laughed, joy and lust filling his eyes. "That's a lot of pressure."

"I'm pretty sure you're good. Judging from what happened just a minute ago, I have no doubts."

He came back to bed, hunching over her, bracing his arms by her shoulders on the mattress. "I live to please you," he teased.

And then Jared got serious. He was definitely an overachiever. Within minutes her entire body had been touched, kissed, caressed and set aflame. She was breathing hard, tingling from head to toe and practically begging for mercy.

Finally, Jared came up over her and settled between her legs, joining their bodies, inching into her cautiously, almost reverently. "Oh, man, Bella. You feel… *so damn good*."

She relished his comment, unable to reply, her heart and her body too caught up in the moment.

And then he began to move. Sensations deep and satisfying filled her, and all she could do was move with him, taking up his rhythm and cadence. They were fluid in motion, striving, pushing, giving to one another. Bella could easily let herself go, but she held back, held on.

Waiting for Jared.

"Are you ready, Bella?" he whispered finally.

She nodded. "For quite a while now."

A chuckle rose from his chest. "Maybe you're not such an angel after all."

"And maybe we're not as different as you'd like to think."

"You could be right."

Then Jared swept her away, taking her to a no-think zone, a place where he proved to her once and for all who the real devil was between the two of them.

And thank goodness for that.

Seven

The morning came quickly, too quickly for her to absorb all that had happened last night. She lay in her own bed, her body sore in all the right places. She'd hated leaving Jared last night, and though he'd begged her to stay, she couldn't leave Sienna alone all night. Besides, it was safer with him downstairs and her living upstairs. It gave her some space, some time away from him to gather her thoughts.

Mostly, she wished she'd met Jared under different circumstances. She wished to high heaven she hadn't had to lie to him and everyone here at Stone Ridge. She wished she wasn't in hiding, that she could've had a normal upbringing with a reasonable father who wasn't always trying to run—and had nearly ruined—her life.

But wishful thinking never got her anywhere.

Instead she turned to the one glorious thing in her life. Sienna. Her daughter's eyes fluttered and she tossed around in the bed. She'd be waking up soon, ready to take on a new day. Sometimes Bella felt it was just her and Sienna against the world.

It was enough. It had to be.

A minute later Sienna's eyes opened and she immediately smiled. For Bella, these waking moments were precious, seeing the light on her baby's face when their eyes connected. "Morning, baby girl."

"Mommy."

Sienna rolled over, nearly on top of her, and squeezed her neck.

"I'm here, Sienna. I always will be."

A tear dripped from Bella's eye. She was emotional today, overly so, and it was fear and doubt and confusion about her future all wrapped up into one tumbling snowball that was picking up speed and growing larger every day.

Being with Jared last night had made all the bad things go away. For a short time he'd made her forget about her problems. But this morning reality set in and she had no idea what to expect when she went downstairs to cook his breakfast.

Fifteen minutes later, after a quick shower for both of them, she dressed Sienna in her favorite cartoon character outfit and put her damp hair up in pigtails, while Bella donned a pair of jeans and a red-plaid shirt. She pushed the sleeves up, ready for work. The two of them headed downstairs to the kitchen.

It didn't appear that Jared was awake yet, which gave

her time to implement her plan. She set Sienna on a blanket on the floor with her ABC blocks and a few of her princess dolls. Cinderella was her favorite. Bella thought it odd that she was in the same situation as the blond-haired fairy-tale princess. With the clock ticking, Cinderella came to the ball magically and quite by accident to spend time with the handsome prince, hiding her true identity and knowing full well her time with him was limited. When would Bella's clock strike twelve?

If there was even a hint her father was closing in, Bella would have to pick up and run. She'd have to leave Stone Ridge, a place where she felt welcome and safe.

She shook those thoughts off, convincing herself she was well hidden at the ranch, and set about making breakfast. In a matter of minutes she had all the ingredients ready and set the oven to bake. Next she cleaned up the mess from last night, washing dishes at the sink.

Suddenly she heard footsteps approaching and before she could turn around, Jared's strong arms wrapped around her from behind and his lips nestled her throat, planting soft kisses there. "Mornin', Bella."

She leaned against the wall of his chest and sighed. "Good morning."

"Did you sleep well after you left me?" he asked quietly.

She nodded. "I did."

"Me, too. Though I missed you."

She'd missed him, too. This was happening so fast and she should be frightened, but right now, pressed against him and feeling his strength, hearing his voice, she felt safe. "I hope you understand why I—"

"Of course I do. Sienna comes first. She always will."

She turned to him then and met his eyes. There was genuine understanding there and something else: the tiniest hint of the future. Or was she reading too much into his comments? "Thank you for—"

His mouth came down on hers for a beautiful good-morning kiss and she forgot her deep thoughts and simply enjoyed being in his arms.

When the kiss ended, she smiled. "I'm glad this isn't awkward or anything."

"Honey, nothing about me and you is awkward. We're kinda seamless, don't you think?"

Before she could absorb that, Jared turned away and hunched down next to Sienna on the floor. "Mornin', sugar plum. What're you playing?"

"Dollies. Pay, Tared?"

"Of course."

Bella scratched her head. Where had Jared Stone come from? He was like a gift from heaven. Was it possible she could be so lucky twice in one lifetime, first with Paul and now Jared?

She walked over to the two of them. "Can Mommy play, too?"

Sienna kept her focus on her doll. Jared was helping her put tiny shimmery shoes on Cinderella's feet. "Pay, Mommy."

Ten minutes later the air filled with a sugary aroma. Jared lifted his nose in the air. "Something smells awfully good."

"It's a surprise."

"A surprise breakfast? Does it have tofu?"

She shook her head. "I promise it doesn't."

"Then I'll be sure to love it." His blue eyes twinkled and her heart sort of melted.

"Prize, Mommy?"

Sometimes she forgot how astute Sienna was. She soaked up knowledge quickly. Her daughter was learning in leaps and bounds. Every day she understood more and more. "Yes, there's a surprise for you, too, Sienna."

When the timer dinged, Bella rose from her spot on the floor. "I'd better get that."

Jared rose, too, and picked up little Sienna. As he held her, Sienna's arm circled his neck and Bella stared at the two of them as if…as if…

"Sienna wants to see the surprise, too. Right, Sienna?" Jared asked.

Her daughter bobbed her head up and down.

Scary joy bubbled inside her at the sight of the two of them. She sighed. "Well, okay then." She grabbed two thick pot holders and opened the oven. Gratified to see how well the surprise had turned out, she lifted the pan from the oven and turned to her audience. "Ta-da!"

"Blueberry pie," Jared said, a big, wide grin on his face.

"Pie, Mommy. I have some?"

"Yes, we're all going to have some. With ice cream, too."

Jared's dark blond brows rose.

"Why not?" She could be adventurous, too, and Sienna deserved a treat after all she'd put her through lately. "We can have dessert for breakfast once in a while, right?"

"Absolutely. It looks delicious."

"I…I hope so. Blueberries aren't in season, so I had to use canned fruit." She set the pie down on the counter to cool.

"I would never know," he said. "Can't wait to dig in."

He leaned over and gave her a kiss on the cheek. "Thank you."

Immediately she glanced at Sienna to see if she had any reaction to Jared kissing her. She did. She leaned forward and, with Jared's guidance, kissed her other cheek. "Tank you."

Sienna grinned. "You're both welcome."

As it turned out, Sienna ate her piece of blueberry pie with French vanilla ice cream while sitting on Jared's lap. He spoon-fed her small bites like a pro.

"I can't remember having a better breakfast," Jared said when they were all finished. "And I'm certain little Sienna here hasn't, either. Pie was delicious."

"I'm glad you both liked it. The thing is, Sienna might be bouncing off the walls soon. Sugar tends to fuel her up."

"Does it now? I might have a solution for that."

"I'm all ears."

He grinned. "Do you trust me?"

She nibbled on her lip. She was having a hard time trusting people lately, other than Amy, who knew all of her secrets. She really had to delve deep to answer him. "What are you planning?"

"Can't tell you. This time, I'm gonna surprise you."

"Me?"

"You and Sienna."

"Well?" He was waiting, his brow furrowing. He seemed to think his question was a simple one. One she'd be able to answer without hesitation. Last night she'd trusted him with her body and he hadn't hurt or disappointed her. Just the opposite: it had been thrilling and crazy-good. But Sienna was a different story. Sienna was the most precious thing in her universe.

Yet she had to admit, Jared had been nothing but gentle, caring and kind to Sienna. She'd be safe with him. "Okay, yes. I trust you."

"Great, meet us outside in ten minutes."

She blinked. "Outside?"

"Yep, and no peeking."

"Jared, what are you doing? Get Sienna down from there this instant." Bella's heart raced, thumping against her chest. She bit down hard on her lower lip as she approached the fence.

Jared sat tall in the saddle on a chestnut mare inside the corral, holding Sienna with one hand wrapped around her body, the other hand on the reins.

"Bella, just look at her. Sienna loves it up here on Sundae."

Her daughter was smiling and, with Jared's encouragement, was stroking the horse's thick mane. "Come on over here, Bella."

Her heart in her throat, Bella stepped up to the fence, noting the joy on Sienna's face and Jared's big, strong hand locked around her. A war battled inside her head. Was she too protective of Sienna? As if *there* was such a thing as being too protective for a first-time mom.

Or was she projecting all of her fears and anxiety on her baby girl?

"Breathe," Jared said to her.

"I am breathing. Hard."

Sienna giggled when the horse twitched and fluttered her mane. Jared's eyes met with Bella's. "Are we good here?"

She nodded, biting her lip once again.

"I'm gonna circle the corral with her. Okay?"

"Be extra careful," she warned.

He tipped his hat, Sienna waving to her as they moseyed off at a slow pace. Bella lifted her hand and wiggled a finger or two, keeping her gaze locked on Sienna, her trembling beginning to disappear as she noted Jared's obvious expertise on the horse.

By the time they reached the far end of the oval corral, Bella was breathing normally. But just as she let down her guard, a gigantic hawk flew out of the trees and swooped down, winging its way just over Sundae's head. The startled horse reared up, her front legs circling the air as she balanced on her hind legs. Jared and Sienna were thrown back on the horse and Sienna's panicked screams pierced the air. Bella shot over the fence and raced toward Sienna. By the time she reached the two of them, she was out of breath. Jared held her crying daughter in his arms, trying to sooth her.

"Give me my baby now," she demanded. She was spitting mad, but didn't want to frighten Sienna so she held her anger inside. "She's scared to death."

Bella reached up and the second Sienna saw her, she nearly flew out of Jared's arms to be comforted by her mother. "It's okay, baby. It's okay." She kissed the top of Sienna's head over and over, holding her close.

"I can't even talk to you right now," Bella said to Jared, unable to look at him.

Jared climbed down off the horse and followed her as she began walking away.

"We were never in any real danger. I would've never let anything happen to her, Bella."

"Jared," she said through clenched teeth. "Please shut up and let me take my baby inside. I don't want to cause a scene and frighten Sienna any more than she already is."

She heard Jared let out a big sigh but, thankfully, he stopped following her. The darn man hadn't even thought about his own injuries and the damage he could've sustained.

She'd been a fool to trust Jared Stone. What the heck had she been thinking?

Jared paced in his study, unable to keep his anger in check, unable to get any work done this morning. Did Bella really think he'd put Sienna in danger? The horse had been spooked, but Jared had never lost control. He'd clamped onto Sienna like a vise until Sundae settled down. It was all over in a split second. He was sorry Sienna got frightened, but she'd stopped crying the instant she was back in her mother's arms.

Yet he'd never wanted to cause Bella any more grief. He'd never wanted to hurt her. She was becoming important to him and this little rift between them wasn't setting well.

His cell phone rang and he grabbed it off his desk to look at the screen. It was his mom. Veronica Stone Kensey wasn't one you could put off. She'd been calling every day or so to check on his recovery while on a trip to the Mediterranean.

Pinching his nose, he let the phone ring one more time before answering. "Hi, Mom."

"Hi, honey. We're finally back from our vacation. I'm in love with the Italian Riviera. And I think I've gained ten pounds. But more about that later. How are you today?"

His mom was sleek and pretty and she never really put on any weight. Her Floridian friends said it was a blessing how she could eat and eat and never gain an ounce. "I'm doing well, Mom. Every day is easier and easier."

"So, you're up and about?"

"Pretty much. I'm working, and today I took Sundae out for a ride." He wouldn't go into details but his mother deserved to hear his progress. He and Cooper had insisted she not come home from her trip when the accident happened. Things could've been a lot worse, but Jared had been lucky and there wasn't much she could have done to help his broken ribs. So as a compromise, they'd agreed to give her updates every day or two. Cooper and Lauren's pregnancy was also a subject of these conversations.

"You're not overdoing it, are you?"

"No, Mom. I know my limitations."

His mother seemed skeptical. She'd never approved of his daredevil streak.

"Okay." She sighed. "I guess I'll be able to see that for myself. I'm coming home for the holiday party at the end of the week." Even though his mom lived in a ritzy retirement village in Florida, she always referred to Stone Ridge Ranch as home. "I'll spend a few days with you, if that's all right?"

His eyes slammed shut. He loved his mother a lot, but her timing wasn't good. "Sure, Mom. I'd love to see you. You're welcome here anytime."

"Thanks, honey. Gosh, it's always so good to hear your voice."

"Same here, Mom. I'm glad you had a good time on your trip."

Jared ended the conversation and ran a hand down his face. With Bella angry at him, he felt at odds with everything, and now he'd have his mother to contend with. She was astute in matters of the heart; one look at him with Bella and his mom would figure out that something was going on between them.

Around lunchtime, he heard Bella being unusually quiet tinkering in the kitchen and he knew what that meant. She didn't want him popping in to watch her cook. That was too damn bad. He needed to iron this out with her or this uneasy feeling in his gut would never go away.

He took a few calming breaths and then marched to the kitchen. Standing in the doorway, he found her at the island chopping onions with a vengeance. "I bet you wish that was my head."

She glanced up and eyed him. "No. Maybe. I don't know."

"Where's Sienna?" he asked, walking into the room.

"Napping. She had quite a morning."

"Blueberry pie and a wild horse ride."

Bella put the knife down. They stood with the granite island between them. "It's not a joke. She was really scared…and so was I."

"I'm not making a joke. I'm sorry, Bella. I never meant for you to be frightened."

"You have no idea what it's like being a single mother. I'm all Sienna has. And she's all I have. I love her beyond belief. And it's my job to protect her."

"Protect her, Bella. Not stifle her."

"Jared, for heaven's sake. She's not even two years old."

"I know that. But I also want you to know that I'd never put her in danger. She was safe the entire time. I'd die rather than have anything happen to her. I can protect her, too."

"You almost did die not too long ago. You can't protect her, not the way I need. You don't see the danger in things. You drive fast, race motorcycles, take too many chances. Almost dying in that accident didn't change you."

Jared put his hands on his hips and stared at her. This conversation was going nowhere.

"Listen, I'm really sorry for making you worry. For scaring Sienna. It won't happen again. I can't take us being angry at each other, Bella. Not after last night. Not with the way I feel about you."

Bella put her head down and her arms braced on the counter began to tremble. Tears dripped from her eyes.

"Ah, Bella." He came around the counter and turned her into his arms. "Don't cry."

"It's the…o-onions," she whimpered.

"It's not the onions," he said softly, brushing away the soft strands of hair falling into her face. "I'm sorry, sweet angel. So sorry. I promise to be more cautious with you and Sienna. Just don't cry anymore."

His plea had the opposite effect and she broke down completely, sobbing into his chest. It was as if all of her troubles had come crashing down on her and all he could do was hold on to her tight, absorb some of her pain. Make her feel safe again.

"Let it out, sweetheart. It's okay. I'm here."

A nibble of curiosity about Bella's background was beginning to grow in his mind. She seemed to be hiding more than her grief, but he wasn't entirely sure about it and now was not the time to question her. Or maybe Jared really didn't understand what she was going through. Maybe, unintentionally, he was making things worse for her.

Finally after a minute, she quieted to a sniffle. "I'm…sorry. I messed up your shirt."

She patted his chest and lifted her soft, sad eyes to his. His heart squeezed tight. "Anytime, Bella. Ruin all my clothes, I don't mind."

The tiniest smile graced her face. She was so pretty, red-nose, swollen eyes and all. Or maybe he was such a goner when it came to her.

"You always say the right thing," she whispered.

Her voice was sweet, touching him in a dozen amazing ways. "I think we had our first fight."

She nodded. "I think we did."

"Kiss and make up?" he asked. He had Bella in his arms and she was soft and pliant and, unless he'd missed something, ready.

She gazed at his mouth, deep longing in her eyes, and he let out a quiet groan. She was vulnerable right now, and he wouldn't take advantage of that, but everything about her seemed to need the exact same thing he needed. To touch, to kiss, to forgive.

"Bella," he whispered right before he claimed her mouth. Both sucked in a breath at the joining of their lips. His heart raced and his body pinged. This woman made him ache. He deepened the kiss, unable to stop, unable to release his hold on her.

She kissed him back gently and then, as if something snapped inside her, desperation seemed to take hold. She gripped his shirt, nearly climbing up his body, demanding more of his kisses, more of him. There was a spark, a connecting energy that couldn't be ignored. It demanded. It crusaded. It conspired to bring them together.

"Forget lunch," he said between fiery hot kisses. "Come with me, Bella." If his ribs had been slightly more recovered, he'd have lifted her into his arms. Instead he put his arm over her shoulder. Her head automatically rested against his chest as they strode to his bedroom.

This time there was no hesitation. No quiet, intimate words. Once inside the bedroom, they climbed upon the bed fully clothed. The clothes were a minor nuisance, something that could be taken care of later.

All that mattered right now was touching each other, kissing, bringing their need and desire to be together, to make up, to give in, to ease the pain that seemed to scar them both.

He touched every part of her through her clothes, kissed her lips, cheeks and chin. The need inside him was strong and potent and so very real, it half scared the life out of him. Nothing much did, but this…this thing between him and Bella was driven and wild and blissfully uncontrollable.

Soon kissing wasn't enough and their clothes were off quickly. He couldn't describe what it was like being skin-to-skin with Bella. It was off-the-charts good. She tasted like sugar all the time, her body so sweet and delicious. He cupped her perfect pert breasts, not large by any standard, but luscious, and suckled one then the other. The little cooing sounds she made were so damn enticing he was halfway to oblivion already.

She nearly finished him off when she circled her hand around his shaft. His hips jolted upward. Surprised and pleased, he leaned back, absorbing the feel of her hand on him, the way she moved, the beautiful vision she made in the minimal light coming into the room as her long black hair streamed down her body.

She *was* his angel, because he was surely in heaven.

"Bella," he breathed. It was on the tip of his tongue to tell her what he was feeling inside, but he held back. It wasn't the time to claim her as his. She deserved better than a bedroom declaration, but he knew in his heart where this was heading.

"Jared, please. I need you."

Oh, man, he needed her, too. It took only a few seconds to sheath himself with protection, and then Bella was straddling him, her olive-skinned body glowing above him. The sight of this woman straddling him, ready to make love to him, would be forever embedded in his mind.

"I'm ready, sweetheart," he said, placing his hands on her hips and guiding her onto him. Their joining stole all his breath. He couldn't utter a sound. She was breathtaking and he was about as turned on as he'd ever been in his life.

They moved in unison, giving and taking. Her pulse-pounding erotic movements spurred his endurance. He never wanted this to end.

But when they'd finally reached the pinnacle of their desire, Jared wasn't sorry. They splintered apart at the same time, drawing out the last fragments of pleasure for each other. Unselfishly giving whatever they had left to please each other.

For Jared, it had been the best, most satisfying, sex in his life.

It was also something else, as well. Bella was systematically erasing Helene's betrayal from his mind and perhaps giving him a second chance at hope and faith and trust.

A little later, Bella lay in Jared's arms. The baby monitor he'd so thoughtfully brought into his bedroom showed Sienna napping soundly. Jared stroked Bella's hair, absently weaving his fingers in and out of the strands.

She cuddled up closer to him, breathing in the scent of his skin, feeling the steady, solid beat of his heart under her palm. She was in a different world when she was with Jared. He made her forget the bad things. It amazed her how quickly she'd become attracted to him, how quickly his presence in the room brightened her day.

Even though she'd been totally pissed at him about his recklessness on the horse, he'd managed to appease her with an apology that had come straight from his heart. Bella believed him to be sincere and earnest. There wasn't a deceptive bone in his body. He was the real deal. Score one for Jared.

Too bad she couldn't say the same about herself.

But she wasn't going to think about that now. These precious moments with him would soon be over when Sienna woke up. Right now, she just wanted to concentrate on being with him, guilt-free. "This is nice," she murmured as he absently stroked her arm, his touch creating tingles.

"It is. The best way to spend an afternoon."

She could hear his smile. "For me, too."

"I never thought…"

He stopped himself from finishing the sentence and she got the feeling it was going to be profound. "You never thought what?"

He sighed deeply and held her a bit tighter. "I never thought I'd ever feel this close to a woman again."

"What does that mean?" she asked quietly.

"It means that my ex really screwed me for relationships. I've been with a few women since, but it was never like this. It never lasted."

She didn't want to think about Jared with another woman…ever. But she needed a few answers. Was he telling her he thought they would last? That his feelings for her were strong enough to overcome whatever his ex had done to him? "She must've hurt you badly."

He kissed the top of her head. "She did."

"How? What did she do, Jared?"

He hesitated a long while and she thought to retract her question. Tell him it didn't matter. Tell him he didn't have to reveal his secret, because she couldn't reveal hers, and already the guilt she experienced was piling up.

But before the words were out, Jared began. "I met Helene in Dallas more than two years ago. She was working as a secretary in my friend's construction office. She was new in town, from this little country in Eastern Europe, and we hit it off immediately. We began dating that summer and things spiraled from there really quickly. I mean, I thought she was the one. I met her brother, she met mine. We were happy. You know, looking back, I see all the red flags, but at the time I was sort of blind. I fell hard for her and asked her to marry me. We were to have a Christmas wedding."

"And then what happened? Did she break it off?"

"No, I did. I surprised her one day at her apartment and walked in on her and her *supposed* brother in bed together. God, I felt like a big idiot. She'd set me up. She'd needed permanent entrance into the country and the man she'd introduced as her brother had really been her lover."

"Wow. That must've been a shock."

"You have no idea."

"Jared, I'm sorry." She lifted up enough to reach his mouth and kissed him.

He smiled. "Don't be. I'm fine, other than it's been sort of hard to trust anyone, you know?"

Pricked by guilt over her lies to him, she sighed. "I do know. Thanks for sharing that with me."

"Hey, I'm okay. But I know you're struggling about some things, too."

She froze. Oh, God, had he picked up on her lies? Was he suspicious? Because she'd saved his life, he'd taken her at her word about who she was. She still didn't think she knew him well enough to reveal her secret. She trusted him with her body, yes. But, she couldn't possibly trust him with Sienna's safety. He was a good guy, but his judgment at times came into question. What had happened today with the horse had sealed her stance on the matter. So as much as she wanted to share her burden with him, her instincts were telling her it was too soon.

"I mean, you've been through so much, losing your husband and raising Sienna."

Her shoulders fell in relief. "I won't lie. It's been difficult. But it's getting better."

"Am I part of your healing?"

"Maybe. Am I part of yours?"

"Hell yeah, you are. The day of the accident, I remember you telling me how lucky I was. I didn't think so at the time, when everything in my body ached. But now I do. Now, thanks to you, I'm lucky enough to ache in different ways."

He kissed her lips quickly and laughed.

"You!" She tossed a pillow at his head and he dodged it.

"Pillow fight," he announced.

"Not right now. I've got to get upstairs. Sienna's restless and bound to wake up soon, but I'll take a rain check on that pillow fight. It could get really interesting." She rose and donned her clothes rapidly. Jared snagged her arm and pulled her in, claiming her lips in one last kiss. A doozy.

And then she was off to see about her daughter, smiling wide in direct contrast with the hefty dose of dread draining into her stomach.

To say she was conflicted was a gigantic understatement.

Eight

The sun was just setting on the Christmas tree farm, the temperature brisk. The whimsical laughter of children filled the air as Bella shopped for the perfect Christmas tree. Jared followed directly behind her, holding a bundled Sienna, the two thick as thieves now.

"How about this one, Sienna?" Bella asked. She pointed to a Douglas fir that rose eight feet in the air.

Sienna tugged on her red-and-white knit cap and giggled. "No."

It had fast become a game.

"No, we don't like it, Mommy," Jared said.

"*You* don't." Bella stomped her feet and pouted. "But I think it's perfect."

Sienna giggled again and shook her head, joy twinkling in her eyes as she and Jared conspired and both chorused, "No!"

Bella laughed at the silliness and they moved on.

They came upon a giant open-air shed decorated with all sorts of multicolored lights, blow-up Santas and snowmen, and pretty wire reindeer. The owners were selling ornaments and tinsel and trees, of course. Hot cocoa and snacks were also available to make the shopping experience even more fun. "Hey, let's get some hot cocoa," Jared suggested. "And maybe a Christmas cookie or two."

"Sounds great," Bella said.

"Okay, I'll be right back." He handed Sienna over to Bella but the baby left his arms quite reluctantly.

"Tared be right back," her daughter repeated.

"Yes, he's coming right back with cookies, sweetie. Don't you worry."

She found a hay bale to sit on and cuddled up next to Sienna, keeping them both warm. But when Jared didn't come back right away, Bella began scanning the grounds, wondering what was keeping him. She spotted the woman first; the neighbor she'd met not too long ago. Johnna stood close to Jared, holding on to his forearm like her life depended on it.

Ripe, unwelcome jealousy slashed through Bella and she took a hard swallow. The two seemed to be laughing about something, the mists of their breaths mingling, and it was like a knife slicing her heart. But she had to come to grips with the fact that she had no real claim on Jared. They hadn't spoken of matters of the heart. What was happening between them was all so new and…and…her life was such a mess right now.

Watching Jared with a woman who wasn't lying to him, a woman who seemed genuinely nice, a woman he had known most of his life, not only confused her but brought her reality back to the forefront. What was she doing with Jared Stone?

Having an affair?

Hiding from her real emotions?

Jared returned shortly after, holding a box of goodies, and noticed her mood immediately. "Sorry, it took longer than I thought," he said, breaking off a small piece of cookie and giving it to Sienna. "Here you go, sugar plum. I ran into my neighbor," he added.

"Hmm, Johnna."

Jared handed her a foam cup of hot chocolate. "Yeah, Johnna. She's all excited."

"I could tell."

Jared shook his head, a cocky smile lifting one side of his mouth. "Hey, no need to be jealous."

"I'm not jealous, for heaven's sake. I have no right to be."

"You have every right to be. I mean, you have no need to be. I mean, what the hell, Bella? You're making me crazy. Before I met you, I wanted nothing to do with Christmas ever again. And now look at me. I'm here having a Christmas experience with you and Sienna, and enjoying myself. Doesn't that tell you something?"

Bella couldn't keep her lips from twitching. "A Christmas experience?" A chuckle escaped.

The heat in his eyes mellowed and he smiled. "Yeah, that's what I said."

"So what's the big news with Johnna?"

"She's getting back with her ex. He's been trying to make things right with her for months and they've finally worked things out. There might be a wedding soon."

"That is good news." Now she felt like Scrooge.

"Bella, you have nothing to worry about. I'm not... going anywhere."

"Because you live here."

He rolled his eyes. "Woman, don't you know how much I care about you?"

She inhaled deeply. "I'm...beginning to."

"Where's mistletoe when you need it?" he asked, leaning in.

"You don't need it, Jared."

And then his lips came down on hers. She closed her eyes and relished the feel of his kiss and the tiny bursts of joy popping around inside her. But too soon it was over and he lifted Sienna and kissed her cheek, too.

Sienna hung her arms around his neck and a glimmer of something beautiful entered his eyes.

He reached into his jacket pocket. "Here, this is for you," he said, handing Bella a gift wrapped in red paper and tied with raffia.

"For me?" she asked.

He nodded. "I just saw it and it reminded me of you."

He took out another gift, one much smaller, and handed it to Sienna. "One for you, too."

Bella untied the bow and opened the paper on the

first gift. It was a Christmas ornament. A gold-rimmed, white-porcelain angel holding a basket of red-and-green flowers in her hands. Written on the angel's wings were the words Joy and Faith.

"This is beautiful, Jared."

"Sienna's is a smaller version. She's an angel, too."

"Thank you," she said, tears welling in her eyes. She helped Sienna open her little package. "Look, Sienna. A baby angel. Can you say 'thank you' to Jared?"

"Tank you." She held on to the angel like it was the most precious gift she'd ever received. "Pretty."

"It is pretty. Let Mommy take care of it for you while you drink your milk." She took the angel out of Sienna's hands and replaced it with a milk bottle.

"Bella, you've brought me joy and helped to restore my faith in life. I know you don't like me saying it, but to me, you and Sienna are angels."

"Jared, you give me too much credit." Holding the ornament in her hand, touched by his generosity and thoughtfulness, she still felt as though she didn't have any right to him, not in a way that mattered.

"You know what?" Jared said, ignoring her comment. "How about we finish our cookies and find a nice big tree to bring home to Stone Ridge."

"I think we can do that."

And they went in search of the perfect tree to decorate with their new angel ornaments.

"Don't let me distract you," Jared said, sitting on a kitchen stool facing her workstation.

Was he kidding? He was a total distraction. It was almost 2:00 a.m. and Bella was hard at work perfecting a new recipe. "That's like saying don't let the sun shine."

She looked away from her notepad to gaze into his gleaming blue eyes. The twinkle in them sped up her heartbeats. Jared, barefoot, wearing a pair of dark sweatpants, filling out a white T-shirt with a solid chest and muscular arms, his hair sleep-tousled… All combined, it was enough to make her forget to add tomatoes in her tomato soup recipe. Not good.

"I can leave, Bella," he said, as if it was the last thing he wanted. "Let you do your work."

It was the *last thing* she wanted, too. "Actually, stay."

"Because I inspire you?" He was teasing.

She smiled and nodded.

A groan lifted from his chest. "Bella."

"I mean, uh, I like having the adult company."

"And I like *being* your adult company."

She smiled, not allowing her mind to go there. If she did, she wouldn't get any work done tonight. "It was awfully nice of you buying a little Christmas tree for the kitchen." She took her eyes off him to view the five-foot Douglas fir sitting in the corner of the room, waiting patiently to be decorated. They'd actually left the tree farm with two trees.

"Sienna spends so much time in here, she should have a tree to enjoy all day. And she can help decorate it."

"That sounds like fun. I think we'll do it in the morning."

"Coffee smells good. Want some?" he asked, rising from his seat. Earlier, she'd set a pot of decaf brewing.

"Sure, thanks."

After a minute he delivered a cup to her. It was amazing how wide-awake they both were. She was used to waking up and cooking during the night. But this would all change soon for Jared. Once he got back to work full-time and began commuting to Dallas, these special nights would probably end.

Jared sat and sipped his coffee. "Tell me about your childhood, Bella."

She stiffened and averted her eyes, pretending to peruse her notes. "Uh, nothing much to tell really. I don't remember my mother. She passed away during childbirth. My baby brother didn't make it, either. At the time, I was just a tot, not much older than Sienna is now, and I had no clue how it had affected my father. Until I got older, that is. I don't think he ever got over the loss. He had trouble being both mother and father to me. We don't get along."

"Sorry. That's rough. My dad died young, too. It sort of made me want to branch out and do everything I've ever wanted to do, like, right away. Before time runs out."

"But maybe, Jared…doing so could actually cause your time to run out faster."

He scratched his head. "You sound like my brother. And mother."

She walked over to him, wrapped her arms around his neck and brought her mouth to his, giving him a solid earth-shaking kiss. "Do I?" she whispered. He reached for her but she swiftly moved away before he could reciprocate.

"Okay, point taken. So tell me more about your life, Bella."

"First, you tell me what sort of extreme sports are waiting for you once you heal completely?" Her question was meant as a diversion, a way to take the focus off her life.

"They're not extreme, Bella. I ride motorcycles. I like fast cars. I race boats during the spring and summer. I've been on long endurance runs on my bike. I've river-rafted and skydived. As soon as I get the word from the doc, I'm gonna take flying lessons."

"Yeah, all normal everyday stuff as safe as, say... going to a movie or hiking a trail."

"You don't approve? Hell, Bella, if you want to go to a movie, I'll take you anytime."

She rolled her eyes. Was he serious? "Jared, you're forgetting I have an investment in you. I'd like to see your life continue, preferably without injury."

"I'm not going anywhere, Bella. You don't have to worry."

Sadness filled her heart. "That's what Paul would tell me. I don't have to worry. And then he died and it hurt for a really, really long time. It still hurts, Jared."

"I know, Bella. I hate to see you hurting." He rose and approached her. "Fact is, it's the last thing I want for you," he said softly. This time when he reached for her, she flowed into his arms. His solid strength surrounded and settled her. It amazed her how easily his touch could do that. Being tucked into Jared's broad shoulders cocooned her in warmth and heat began to grow in her belly.

He tenderly kissed her forehead and lifted her chin. She looked into his blue eyes, blazing with heat and hunger, and she couldn't fight it any longer. She knew what it was like to be with Jared now, to be joined with him flesh-to-flesh. He was a beautiful man, flawed in only one way: his love for speed and danger. Could she overlook her doubts and open her heart fully to him?

A deep plea rose from her throat. "Jared."

It was a call to him. To take her. To be with her. To make love to her the way he had last night.

"I'm here, angel." And then he lifted her into his arms. The move didn't seem to strain him or to hurt him in any way. "And you don't have to worry."

Jared held her tight, her head resting on his bare chest. They'd made love just a few minutes ago and Bella's body was still humming like a sweet bird. There was nothing selfish in the way they pleasured each other. Jared worked his magic on her, hitting all her sensitive points, making her whimper. And she was beginning to discover what he liked her to do to him, with her mouth, her hands. Which seemed to be pretty much anything she wanted. His wild responses to her, his deep guttural groans, gave her a sense of power and command in bed. She loved pleasing him.

Earlier, Jared had mentioned his mother's visit, but she hadn't had a chance yet to ask him about it. "So, your mother is coming on Friday?" Bella whispered, wondering what her role would be once she got here. She stroked Jared's chest with the palm of her hand, absorbing the feel of him. Already, tingles of awareness were plotting against her tranquility.

"Yeah, she's anxious to see me. I've spoken with her on the phone, but with the party and all, she wants to be here."

"I can understand that. She has to see you for herself. You may be all grown up and resilient, but you're still her boy."

"Boy?" He grinned. "I'll show you boy," he said, rising up. He planted his mouth on hers and kissed her senseless. The heat of his palm covered her derriere and he gave it a long, proprietary squeeze.

She could easily give in to him again—she wanted to—but this was important. She gave him a shove, startling him, and he landed back on the bed. "Jared, we're having a serious conversation here." She smiled.

"We are? I thought we were going to—"

She covered his mouth, stopping his next words. They turned her on and he knew it. "Later. Right now, tell me about your mother."

Jared sighed. "She's as good a mom as we could've ever asked for. Cooper and I put her on a pedestal, continuing in my father's footsteps. He adored her and made us see how wonderful she was every day of our lives. We always knew our mom was on our side when it came to the really important things. She's smart and fun to be around. I guess that's why, when she met Grant six years ago, Cooper and I didn't stand in the way of her getting remarried. Once we scoped him out, that is, and figured out he was worthy."

Bella was floored by his admission. The Stone boys

were protective of their mother. "Wow. She's lucky to have you both."

"Yeah, I guess so."

What would it have been like to have a mother who loved you unconditionally and a father who supported your wishes and stood behind your decisions? She'd had neither, but she wasn't going to have a pity party over it. She'd come to grips with her situation a while ago, but still, every so often, she would fantasize about growing up in a normal, loving household.

That's what she desperately wanted for Sienna.

She touched Jared's cheek, scrutinizing his profile. Was he the man who could make that happen? Was Jared Stone the one?

He lifted her hand to his mouth and kissed it. "My mom's gonna like you, Bella."

"I hope so."

"I know so."

"I've been working with Marie and Lauren a bit on the party. Now that I know your mom is coming, I'm getting a little nervous."

"Why?"

She shrugged. "I don't know. I guess if I were in total control, it might be different. But I wasn't asked to cook anything."

He turned his head to look into her eyes. "Are you upset about that?"

"No. Just curious."

"We've used the same caterers every single year. And…well, to be honest, I don't want you working that night."

"Because the party is mainly for your employees?"

Jared's eyes grew wide. "Is that what you think? Hell, woman. I don't want you behind the scenes because I want you by my side. You and Sienna."

"Like a date?"

"Yeah, like a date."

She stared at him for a long while. Was he dense? And then finally he shook his head, as if shaking out cobwebs.

"Uh, sorry. I should have asked you formally."

"Well?"

"Bella, will you be my date for the Stone Family Christmas party?"

It was really ridiculous how giddy she was about this. Here they were, buck naked in each other's arms after having mind-numbing sex, and Jared was asking her on a date.

"Yes, of course. Sienna and I would be happy to be your date."

"Great. It's settled then."

"Yes, settled."

Jared's hand wandered to her backside again and this time she didn't shove him away. This time she was eager and ready for whatever pleasure they could bring each other.

The next morning, in the privacy of her bedroom, Bella picked up her phone and texted her friend.

Miss you, Amy. How are you?

Amy was attached to her phone by the hip and she texted back right away.

I'm good. What about you? Any news? How's the hunky cowboy?

She made a goofy face at the reference. Jared was fine. As in FINE. She smiled.

All is good here. No problems. What about you? Has anyone else come around looking for me?

No, thank goodness. But I did speak with your father. He's persistent. I led him astray, I think. Told him you might've gone to Oregon to visit Miranda Davies. He shouldn't think you're in the Dallas area. I hope.

Oh, wow. Miranda was a high school buddy. Her father barely knew any of her friends. He'd never taken an interest. He'd always been too wrapped up in his company.

Brilliant. Thank you. Call you when I get a minute.

She ended the message with half a dozen purple-heart emojis and released the breath she'd been holding. If Amy was right, her father wouldn't be looking for her in Texas, which bought her a good deal of time.

Marco thought her an unfit mother, but if she held down a job long enough to prove she was providing a good life for Sienna, his case against her wouldn't stand a chance. At least, that's what she believed after doing extensive research on the subject. And then with that issue settled, she could look to the future and dream her dream again of opening up a restaurant. She was taking baby steps now, but with larger leaps to come.

A few minutes later she put Sienna in a pale blue jumper and pulled her hair back in two big bows, getting her ready to go down and decorate the Christmas tree. Sometimes she'd look at Sienna and simply melt. The maternal need to protect her overpowered Bella at times. She was living a big fat lie to keep her safe. It was necessary, but along with it came tremendous guilt. It had crossed her mind several times to trust Jared. Would she have the nerve to tell him the truth? God, she wanted to. She didn't like lying to anyone, especially Jared. He was becoming truly important in her life.

She was scared…about losing Sienna, and that fear kept her mouth buttoned up tight. She kept telling herself when the time was right, she'd tell him.

Bella dressed in a pair of black slacks and a flowery blouse to offset the cold, dreary day outside. She put her hair half up and secured it with a pretty clasp to keep the strands out of her eyes while she cooked breakfast.

Halfway out the door with Sienna in her arms, she stopped up short. "Whoops. We can't go down without our angels." Bella opened the dresser drawer and handed Sienna hers. "Here you go. Hold on to it carefully. It's very special. Mommy's got hers, too."

"Angel, Mommy." She grasped her ornament with as much care as an almost-two-year-old could possibly manage.

As they descended the stairs and approached the kitchen, the sound of female voices reached Bella's ears. She slowed her pace and stood in the doorway. She found Marie serving coffee to a pretty brunette woman, her eyes as deep and blue as Jared's.

"Come in, Bella," Marie said, waving her inside the kitchen. "Come meet Jared's mother."

The woman stood and smiled. Dressed impeccably in beige slacks and a soft, silk blouse, her face sunny and bright, she put out her hand. "I'm Veronica. So glad to meet you."

"I'm Bella. Very nice to meet you, too," she said, hiding her confusion. Jared's mother wasn't due until tomorrow.

"Yes, Bella. And this must be Sienna." Veronica focused on the baby with delight in her eyes. "Hello, Sienna. I hear nothing but sweet things about you."

Sienna turned away, burying her head on Bella's shoulder. "She's a bit shy with new people."

"I understand. Gosh, it's been years, but Cooper was like that, too. She's adorable."

"She's a good girl," Marie added.

"Thanks, Marie. She has her moments, though."

"They all do," Veronica said. "You never know what little bits of mischief they will get into." She glanced at the ornaments in their hands. "Were you going to decorate the tree?"

"Oh, uh, yes we were, after I make breakfast."

"No need," Marie said. "I made Veronica some toast and coffee when she arrived. That's all she ever likes to have in the morning."

"I'll remember that."

"Jared has no idea I'm here," Veronica said. "After speaking to him last night, I got overly anxious to see him so I changed my flight. Booked a red-eye and well…" She threw her arms up in the air. "Here I am."

Bella smiled.

"Tared?" Sienna asked, looking around for him.

"He's still sleeping, little one," Marie said. "He'll be down in a few minutes, I'm sure."

Bella set Sienna down and she wandered over to the unadorned tree. "Are you sure I can't get you something else to eat?" she asked Veronica.

"Not a thing. But what you can do for me, if it isn't too strange, is let me give you a big hug. You saved my son's life."

She blinked. "Oh, um, sure."

Veronica stepped up and brought her into a gentle embrace. "Thank you from the bottom of my heart," she whispered. "I can never repay you for what you did, but if you ever need anything, please let me know." Veronica backed away, giving her a sincere look. "Okay?"

"Okay, but you don't owe me anything. I'm only glad I was there to help."

"So am I. When I think of what might have happened…never mind. I won't nag him…much." Veronica wiggled her brows and Bella laughed.

Veronica scrutinized her face for a second. "You kind of remind me of someone I know. But I can't quite place it."

Bella froze. Her heart began to pound. "Do I?"

Veronica nodded. "You do. Maybe it'll come to me."

She turned her attention to Sienna, who was munching on a cracker Marie had given her. "So tell me, how old is Sienna?"

They spent the next ten minutes talking about babies, the joys and frustrations of raising children. Veronica was super excited to become a grandmother for the first time. She was planning on surprising Cooper and Lauren next this morning. She was so easy to talk to, Bella passed off her earlier comment. She knew for a fact she'd never met Veronica Stone, so it was probably nothing. She was being too paranoid about things. She had to lighten up. Amy had pretty much assured her she had nothing to worry about with Marco.

"Angel, Mommy."

"Yes, I know, sweet girl. Excuse us," she said to Marie and Veronica. Sienna ran over to the tree and just then Bella spotted Jared in the kitchen doorway, his shirt undone, his jeans riding low on his waist, the face she'd kissed a hundred times shadowed with a day-old beard. She gasped as his eyes found hers and then his mother stepped into her line of vision.

"Hi, honey."

"Mom, you're here." He blinked a few times. "Am I dreaming?"

She glanced at Bella and then back at him. "Actually, you do look a little dreamy-eyed."

His mother was astute. A warm rush of heat climbed up Bella's throat.

Veronica walked into Jared's arms. "So good to see you, son. I've been worried about you. I hope you don't mind me surprising you this way."

"No, Mom. It's good to see you, too." They separated after a few seconds and Jared stepped back, buttoning his shirt. "Have you met Bella and Sienna?"

"I have. We were getting to know each other when you walked in."

"That's good. Did you travel all night?"

"Just half the night. But it's worth it to see you looking so healthy. I bet Bella has something to do with that."

"Bella?" Jared nearly croaked.

"Marie tells me she's an amazing chef, all healthy food apparently. Is that right, Bella?"

"Yes, uh, that's right."

"Well, I'm happy you're here," Veronica said. She gave her son another glance, one he may have deliberately ignored.

Walking farther into the room, he picked up a piece of toast from the table and chewed for a moment. "You want to put your angel on the tree, sugar plum?"

Sienna nodded.

"Let's do it." He smiled at his mom, then strode to the tree and bent next to Sienna. "Where do you think it should go?"

Sienna looked at the tree then ruffled a few branches until she found her spot. "Tere."

"I think that's a very good place for it."

Hand in hand, he helped Sienna hook the ornament onto a branch. "Wow, Sienna. You did it."

"I did it," she parroted.

Bella clapped her hands. "Good girl. I'm so proud of you."

Sienna's face beamed.

Veronica and Marie smiled, too.

"Babies bring so much joy into the home," Veronica said.

Then she looked straight at Jared with knowing eyes.

Jared sat for dinner at Cooper's house, breaking bread with his brother and his wife and, of course, his mother.

"Too bad Bella couldn't come," Lauren said. "I invited her and little Sienna."

"You did? She didn't mention it." It was news to Jared. His mother had insisted on all the family being together. It happened too rarely and he hadn't been about to disappoint her by not showing up.

Lauren was feeling great these days, having passed some pregnancy milestone that meant no more nausea or exhaustion. She was almost five months along now. And to think Coop had almost blown it with Lauren, plotting a scheme to stop her wedding to her sleazy fiancé. All during that time, Coop never planned on falling in love with her. Now Coop was married and going to be a father. There was no doubt he would make a damn good one.

"Maybe Bella needed a night off," Cooper said.

"It sounded more like she didn't want to impose," Lauren said. "Even though I insisted she wouldn't be. She did me a big favor today and I feel bad I didn't press her harder to come by."

Jared scratched his chin. He wanted Bella here and

was at a loss without her. But it hadn't been his place to invite her. "What did you ask her to do?"

"You'll see. It's a surprise," Lauren answered.

He'd spent a good amount of time catching up with his mother today, and while she'd rested this afternoon he'd finished up on the day's work and hadn't seen Bella after that.

"She seems like a lovely girl," Veronica said, giving Jared another one of her expectant looks.

What did she want him to say? That he was falling for his personal chef? Hell, it was true. Bella was unlike any other woman he'd ever met. And that was a good thing. Instead of revealing his feelings, he simply nodded. "Seems to be."

Lauren put a delicious rib roast on the table with white potatoes, creamed asparagus and biscuits and gravy. No salad, no fresh fruit. And the veggie that was smothered in heavy sauce.

He smiled. Bella would be analyzing this meal and figuring out a way to make it healthy, substituting things and completely removing others. He was getting used to eating her way...healthy with cauliflower everything.

"Are you in la-la land or something, bro? You're smiling silly."

"Am I?"

Lauren eyed him. "Yes, you are."

"I'm feeling fit. Got an appointment on Tuesday with the doctor and I'm hoping he'll give me the okay to get back to my life as usual."

"That's wonderful, Jared," his mother said. "I hope so."

"Yeah, it's been hard doing all the heavy lifting with the company," Cooper added, winking at his wife.

"Don't be an ass, Coop. You know darn well I've been holding up my end." He'd been putting in some useful hours in his office and keeping up his part, when he wasn't playing with Sienna or admiring her mother.

"Is that what you call it? I thought you were playing house."

"Boys!" His mother was only half kidding in her reprimand.

"Playing house? Coop, watch your mouth." Jared's pitch elevated. "You have no idea what Bella has been through."

Everyone's head snapped up and three pairs of eyes stared at him. His protective instincts had kicked in. When Bella and Sienna were involved, he couldn't seem to help it. But now he faced the more than curious scrutiny of his family. How could he answer their questions about his relationship with Bella when he still had so many of his own?

"Hey, sorry," Cooper said. "I meant no disrespect. Bella's great and that kid of hers is a doll."

"She is that," Veronica said. "I like them both, Jared."

"I do, too," Lauren added. "She's doing a great job as a single mom. Actually, I don't know how she does it, balancing work and raising a child without having a husband around to pick up the slack. It's got to be hard. But Bella seems to be working it all out." Lauren placed a hand on her belly bump. "I only hope I can do as good a job."

Cooper leaned over and kissed her forehead. "You'll be a great mom, Laurie Loo. I have no doubt."

"Neither do I," his mother added. "You're a nurturer by nature, Lauren. I only wish you'd tell us what you're having, so Grammy-to-be can do some fun shopping."

Cooper gave his wife a cocky smile. "Shall we?"

Lauren nodded. "We've kept you in suspense long enough."

"Yeah, we wanted the family together when we do our baby's gender reveal."

"Oh, my, you're gonna tell us tonight?" His mother's face lit up.

Lauren rose from the table. "As soon as I clear up the dishes."

"Sit down and don't touch a plate," Cooper said. "I'll clean up."

"I'll help," Jared said.

The two of them made fast work of clearing the table and bringing everything into the kitchen. As they were setting the plates down, Cooper turned a serious eye to him. "You really like that girl, don't you?"

Jared nodded. "I do. She's…she's…"

"I get it. You know, I was just teasing you earlier. You're my kid brother and I want to see you as happy as I am. You deserve it."

"Wouldn't know it by the way you harp on me."

"Nah, don't worry about that. It's my way of getting back at you for scaring the skin off my hide. Man, that accident was really bad. But promise me one thing, Jared. You won't go confusing your gratitude to Bella for the real thing. I mean, we're all indebted to her, but you've got to work through your issues before you can commit. You know what I mean?"

"What if I told you I'm working through those issues with Bella's help?"

"You're sure?"

He nodded. "I'm getting there."

Cooper slapped him on the back. "Then I'm happy for you, bro. Like I said, you deserve it. Now, let's get back inside. We've got the baby's gender to reveal."

Jared walked into the dining room, Cooper behind him holding a chocolate cake on a pedestal server. "Dessert," he announced, "compliments of Bella Reid."

"She made that? It's beautiful," his mother said. "But when do we get to find out if it's a boy or a girl?"

"Right now, Mom." Cooper handed his mother a long cake knife. "Do the honors. The color of the cake inside will give you the answer."

Tears welled in his mother's eyes. "I consider it an honor." She glanced at everyone first, then put the knife into the center of the cake and drew out the first piece.

"Pink!" His mother exclaimed. "It's a girl!" She bounced up and down in her chair like a small child and then rose to kiss both Cooper and Lauren.

Jared grinned and shook his brother's hand and then walked over to hug Lauren. "Congrats, you two."

"Thanks," she said. "It's finally out in the open. We're having a girl!"

"Yeah, too bad your mom couldn't be here. Cooper said she was out of town this week."

"She's in Louisiana for the week visiting a friend, but we found a way. She's on FaceTime now." Lauren looked into the cell phone and waved. "Hi, Mama. Wish you were here with us."

"Me, too, honey. Oh, sweetheart, you're having a girl. I'm very excited. Be sure to save me a piece of that pink cake."

"We'll do that, Mama."

When all the hoopla died down and the final details of the Christmas party were discussed, Jared and his mother said their goodbyes and drove off. He was dying to see Bella, to tell her how sweet it was of her to bake the cake for Lauren and Cooper. To tell her he'd missed her. He glanced at his mother behind the wheel of his car, and shook his head.

With his houseguest, this evening, there would be no rendezvous with his Midnight Contessa.

Instead it was going to be a long, lonely night.

Nine

Bella stood at the top of the stairs, dressed in a snow-white, knee-length, tailored dress adorned with a red-ribbed belt with a matching poinsettia bow to her side. Her shoes matched, too. The only jewelry she wore was a pair of sterling-silver chandelier earrings. Sienna was dressed in Christmas plaid, the dress flaring out in poufy layers, shiny black Mary Janes on her feet.

They were ready for the Christmas party.

"Okay, Sienna. Remember, best behavior, sweet girl. This is your first Christmas party," she said as she held Sienna's hand and started down the staircase.

Jared stood at the bottom of the stairs, dressed in a black suit, looking sharp and crisp and deadly handsome.

She'd missed him these past couple of nights. And she was eager to be his date for the party. Veronica sidled up next to Jared at the bottom of the staircase, and she also watched them descend. There was a point when Jared's mother looked at her and flinched, and then she seemed to recover, leaving Bella with an odd sensation before Veronica walked off.

"You look beautiful, Bella," Jared said. He touched her hair, a sweet, innocent touch that sent shivers up and down her spine. "I like your hair like that." She'd pushed all of it to one side, letting it drape down her chest. It was held in place with a long silver clip.

Then Jared bent to Sienna. "Sugar plum, I don't think there's a prettier girl here. Give me five."

Sienna giggled and slapped at Jared's hand. Sometimes she made it, sometimes she missed. Tonight she made it and her chest puffed out.

"That's my girl."

Jared rose and took Bella's hand.

"This place is really transformed," she said.

"Thanks in part to you."

"Just a small part. I helped with the decorations."

They strolled around the warm, cozy house, two big, blazing fires in the fireplaces keeping the cold December air away. The two trees were decorated with colorful bulbs and ornaments and garland. Christmas music played and Sienna danced about.

Jared introduced Bella and Sienna to many of the ranch hands, workers and their families who kept the ranch going. There were many small children present and Sienna made fast friends with a few of them. Bella also met some of Jared's associates from his Dallas office. All in all, there were about fifty people.

"Champagne?" he asked, grabbing two flutes from one of the wait staff.

"Sure, thanks."

He put his arm around her waist and brought her up close, so they were hip to hip. "God, I miss you," he whispered in her ear.

She swallowed hard. It was the first time he'd touched her in public like this for all the world to see. Heat rose up her neck. She was his date, but she hadn't expected any real show of affection from him in front of his crew and friends. After all, she was his employee.

She whispered back, "Do you really think this is wise?"

"Wise? I think we're beyond being wise, Bella. I'm falling for you and I don't care who knows it. Do you?"

His declaration caught her off guard. God yes, she was falling for him, too. She was too floored to do anything but nod.

"Good. Look up."

She lifted her eyes to find a thick bunch of mistletoe hanging from the ceiling. And when she tilted her head back down, Jared's lips were there, kissing her lightly but with enough potency to set her body on fire.

She scanned the room to see if anyone noticed and found Veronica's eyes on her for a split second before she shifted her attention to the person she was conversing with. Bella's gut clenched and she was suddenly ice cold inside. She shivered.

"Hey, if you're cold, let's go stand by the fire," Jared said. "I think Sienna would like it, too." Jared gathered up her daughter, tempting her with a candy cane, and the three of them entered the parlor and stood by a crackling fire.

"The caterers will be putting out dinner soon," he said. "Are you two hungry?"

"I hungry," Sienna said, sucking on the candy cane.

"Not just for candy, sugar plum." Jared tickled her and she burst out in sweet laughter.

The sound was enough to put joy back into Bella's heart, even though her stomach felt queasy. "I could eat a little something," she said, plastering on a smile.

"Good, because later we might just have Christmas carolers come by the house. And who knows, maybe one of Santa's elves might be stopping by, too."

"Sounds like fun," Bella said, reaching for Sienna and taking her out of Jared's capable arms. She needed to hold her daughter tight to help the uneasy feeling in her gut disappear. Holding Sienna tight always seemed to work.

Yet her mind kept going back to Veronica. Bella scoured her memory, trying to think if she'd said anything to Jared's mother that would upset her. They'd been on friendly terms these past couple of days as they got the house ready for the party. And Veronica had been complimentary of the dishes she'd cooked for all of them.

So what was going on? And why was Veronica avoiding her?

The last of the partygoers was gone now and the caterers and cleanup crew were working hard to get the house back in order. Sienna had managed to keep her eyes open during the festivities, fascinated by the lights and activity, the carolers who'd come inside the house to sing their Christmas tunes and, of course, seeing one of Santa's helpers. Sienna hadn't been brave enough to sit on his lap, but she did receive a toy, a baby doll she'd clutched in her arms the rest of the night. Now Bella was heading up to bed with Sienna fast asleep in her arms.

"Bella, wait." Jared approached the staircase. "Let me take her up for you."

She hesitated only a second. "Okay, thanks." She made the transfer easily and Jared followed her up. She walked into the adjoining bedrooms and quickly turned down the sheets on the bed. She and Sienna had been sleeping together and, at some point, her little girl would get a bed of her own, but these conditions were fine temporarily.

Jared laid her down and Bella carefully removed her shoes and changed her into her pajamas. She tucked her in and kissed her forehead. Jared bent to do the same, and Bella blinked back tears. It was a ritual she and Paul would do together. She wasn't saddened by the gesture but rather hopeful and touched that Jared cared so deeply about her daughter. She walked him to the door and whispered, "Thank you. It was a lovely party."

"Our first date." She smiled and he wrapped his arms around her waist and pulled her close. "I'll miss you tonight."

He nuzzled her hair and then claimed her lips, the kiss going long and deep. They were both breathing hard when the kiss ended. "I'd better go." He sighed and backed away from her.

"Yes, you'd better," she whispered back, feeling the same longing she witnessed in his eyes. They were both aware his mother's room was just down the hall.

"Good night."

"'Night," he said and then he was gone.

Bella walked around in a daze, her heart spilling over with emotion, her lips still tingling from Jared's kiss. She was in love with him. She had no doubt. In the short time she'd known him, he'd become important to her. Every time he walked into the room, her heart just about stopped. She had come to cherish their midnight encounters, as well. Making love with Jared was amazing, but it was more than that. She shared her love of cooking with him, and had his full support. Those late nights had come to mean so much to her.

Five minutes later, as she was brushing her hair, a soft knock woke her out of her thoughts.

Her heart pumped faster at the thought of seeing Jared again.

She opened the door quiet as a mouse and found Veronica standing on the threshold. She gave Bella a small smile. "Can we talk?"

"Uh, yes. Sure. Just let me get the baby monitor."

Veronica waited and then led Bella to a sitting area, a little alcove in the hallway comfortable for two. "Is this all right?"

Bella nodded, her stomach beginning to ache. So she hadn't been wrong, something was up with Veronica and she was about to find out what it was.

"I won't beat around the bush, Bella. Or should I say

Francesca? I know who you are. What I don't understand is why you are lying to my son."

Bella bit her lip and put her head down. Her eyes burned and she struggled to keep from crying. "You're right. I am lying to Jared. But it's not what you might think."

"Honestly, I don't know what to think. When I saw you coming down the stairs tonight, dressed like you are now, I remembered a brief meeting with a young woman who wore her clothes with poise and grace, whose long, dark hair was styled like yours tonight. A beautiful young woman with striking green eyes."

"We've met? I don't remember."

"You wouldn't really, I suppose. You see, before Grant retired, my husband owned a small chain of restaurants and we were at a charity dinner in San Francisco. It must've been…oh, about five years ago. Your father, Marco, was one of the main benefactors and you were with him. I know I'm not wrong. I've since checked you out on the internet. Granted, you weren't in the public eye much, but I did find a link between you and Forte Foods."

"I'm sorry, Veronica. I'm not hiding my identity for any nefarious reasons. I'm trying to keep Sienna safe."

"Care to explain?"

Bella had no choice. She'd been caught red-handed and a big part of her was glad to unburden her secret. For some reason Veronica, although a mother hen with her boys, also had a compassionate streak and seemed willing to hear her out. "Yes, of course. You see, I didn't have a traditional childhood. My mother died when I was just a tot and my father…"

Bella explained everything, leaving nothing out. She told Veronica of her struggles with her father from an early age, of his smothering her, trying to run her life. She explained how she'd defied him when she'd married Paul and then refused to work at the company. Then, while she was still grieving, her father had pushed Ben Tolben on her. He was a very nice man who worked for Forte Foods. They'd had a few dates, but it was never serious and it never could be, yet Marco leaked to the press that they were getting engaged and it had all escalated after that. She concluded with describing the fight that had driven her from San Francisco, fearing that she'd lose her child.

Veronica asked a few questions and seemed satisfied with her answers, but she still wasn't ready to dismiss her lying to Jared. "Why didn't you tell Jared this?"

"I…I couldn't. I haven't been able to trust too many people in my life, especially when it comes to Sienna's safety. She's all I have in this world right now. The thought of her being taken away from me, well…I can't even think about it without feeling sick to my stomach. I…was too scared. So, yes, I'm hiding out here, but I can assure you, what I feel for Jared is very real."

"Yet you couldn't trust him?"

"T-this hasn't been e-easy for me," she whispered. "I'm not a liar by nature." Bella glanced at the monitor she held in her lap. Sienna was sleeping soundly, and tears formed in her eyes seeing her beautiful child looking so peaceful. There wasn't anything she wouldn't do for Sienna. If it meant leaving Jared and Stone Ridge Ranch, she'd do it. She'd pack up her belongings and go, because keeping Sienna with her was her first priority. "I'm protecting my daughter."

"And I'm protecting my son. You understand. I assume you know about Helene and the number she did on Jared?" She shook her head. "I can't let that happen to him again. He's a good man."

"I know," Bella said. "He is good. I care for him very much."

Veronica closed her eyes briefly and drew a breath. "You have to know how appreciative I am that you saved my son's life. And because of that, and the debt I owe you, I'm not going to tell Jared what I know."

"Thank you," Bella said softly, overwhelmed with gratitude and relief.

"But I am going to insist that you do. Bella, you have to promise me you will tell him the truth, the sooner the better. If you don't, I'll be back here next week for Christmas and I won't keep my mouth shut. You understand as a parent, I can't let my son be led astray."

"I'm not doing that. And yes, I promise you, I will tell him."

"Sooner rather than later?"

"Yes, I'll…I'll try to find the right time."

Veronica took her hand and gently squeezed. Her eyes softened in understanding. "Bella, don't wait too long."

"I promise, Veronica." Several tears trickled down her face. This wasn't an easy conversation and she surely didn't want Jared's mother to think the worst of her. She'd keep her promise and tell Jared the truth—and hope she wouldn't lose the man she loved. "I'll tell him soon."

* * *

Bella hardly got a wink of sleep, and in the morning rose from bed exhausted and perplexed. She caught her reflection in the dresser mirror and groaned. It was not a pretty sight. Her body ached, probably from tossing and turning. All night, she'd rehearsed what she would say to Jared and how she would implore him not to see what she'd done as a total betrayal. She'd have to make him see that, just like him, trust didn't come easily to her. He should understand that.

She'd lay it all on the line and tell him what was in her heart and hope that would be enough. Up until this point, he seemed to be a reasonable man. Well, except for his crazy need for speed and danger. While he was recuperating, she really hadn't seen that side of him, but she'd heard enough from his mother and brother about it, and how could she forget the accident?

She shook off the image and glanced down at her baby daughter on the bed. Just gazing at her angelic face was enough to make her forget all the bad stuff in her life. But Sienna's nose was running and she looked pale and clammy this morning.

Bella immediately climbed back on the bed and laid her palm flat on Sienna's forehead. The baby felt warm. Sneezing in her sleep, she nearly woke herself up, but Bella immediately tucked her in more cozily with the blanket.

Once she was sure Sienna was asleep, she walked into the other bedroom and texted Jared.

Sienna isn't feeling well this morning. May have a fever.
I won't be down to make breakfast. Sorry.

She climbed back into bed with Sienna to keep
a good eye on her, and not two minutes later heard
soft knocking at her door. She padded to the door and
opened it only inches.

Jared stood there, dressed in his usual jeans and blue
chambray shirt, face unshaved and hair unruly. Her
heart skipped but she was too concerned about Sienna
to think about anything else. Still, Jared's presence just
had a way of disrupting her normal breathing patterns.
"What's wrong with the baby?" he whispered immediately.

"I'm not sure," she answered, keeping her voice low.
"She was fine last night. And this morning her nose is
running and I think she has a fever."

"You think?"

"Yes, she's warm, but my baby thermometer is broken, so I'm not sure. Sorry about breakfast."

He waved her off. "There's enough leftovers to feed
my entire crew. Don't worry about cooking today."

"Thank you."

"So besides a baby thermometer, what else does she
need?"

"That's it. I think I have everything else."

"Let me see what it looks like. I'll make sure you
get a new one."

"Okay," she whispered. "Give me a sec."

She went into the bathroom and returned right away,
showing Jared the thermometer. "This is it."

He took it out of her hands. "I'll have a new one delivered from the pharmacy in town."

She stared into Jared's concerned eyes. Gosh, he really cared about Sienna. If Bella blew it with him, it might be the biggest mistake of her life. "Thank you."

He nodded. "Just keep that sugar plum healthy, will you?"

The baby slept most of the day and Bella managed to get some rest, too. Sienna had no appetite really, only munching on baby crackers and sipping from her bottle. The thermometer Jared had delivered from the pharmacy registered a low-grade fever, which meant Sienna's body was fighting off an infection.

Bella got up to shower and change her clothes. She took her computer to the other room and began going over her notes. She was in the middle of designing a different version of a Christmas morning soufflé when Sienna began coughing. The cough was rough, coming from deep in her chest, and nothing Bella had ever heard before. She raced over to her and sat her up immediately, holding her until the coughing fit was over. And then Bella touched her face. "Oh, no, Sienna." The baby was burning up.

She raced to the door and called down for help. "Jared! Marie!"

Sienna's hacking returned. It was deep and guttural, like barking.

Bella heard Jared's footsteps on the stairs and the sound put her a little bit at ease. She needed him right now. "What's wrong, Bella?"

"It's Sienna. She's burning up and the cough… it's horrible. I think she's wheezing. She's not getting enough air."

He walked over to Sienna and the frightened look in his eyes added to her own fear, but his voice was calm as he picked up the phone. "I'll call Lauren. She'll know what to do."

Bella stayed with Sienna, encouraging her to drink between her coughing fits. The wheezing got worse, and raw panic seized Bella's stomach. Her baby wasn't breathing right.

Jared hung up the phone and strode over to the bathroom. "Bella, while I get the shower going, you get Sienna and hold her on your lap on the toilet seat. We need the room to steam up real fast."

She didn't have time to question him. She did as he asked, picking up the baby and bringing her to the bathroom. He closed the door behind them.

"We need Sienna to breathe in the steam until she's back to normal. Lauren is pretty sure it's croup. It means a ride to the hospital later, but only once we're sure the steam is reducing the swelling in her throat. That's what's causing the wheezing."

"Should we call the paramedics?"

"We could but, honestly, Stone Ridge is so remote, it'll be faster to drive her to the hospital ourselves. And Lauren says not to be scared. She's calling ahead to our local hospital. It's small but efficient and this way they'll be waiting for her."

"Okay, okay." Her own breathing nearly stopped, but she trusted Jared's instincts on this.

"Encourage her to breathe in and out."

The room steamed up pretty fast and they sat there for long minutes as the baby began to breathe easier and easier.

Sienna seemed confused about all of it, but her cough wasn't as bad as before and her breathing seemed much better. It was time to go.

Jared helped dress the baby in warm clothes and then tossed Bella her jacket. "Put this on. Mommy doesn't need to get sick, too."

Jared picked up Sienna. "You ready?"

"Yes, let's get her checked out."

Outside, as they approached her car, a light rain started to fall. Jared put his hand out for her keys.

"You can't drive," she said.

"I'm driving, Bella. You need to get in the back seat and see to your daughter. There isn't time to argue. It's raining and, besides, I know where I'm going. I'll get us there faster."

She stared at him.

"Safely."

He'd read her mind. But, honestly, her nerves were too jumpy for her to drive anyway. She dumped the keys into his hands. "Okay. Let's go."

Jared paced back and forth outside the triage room. Bella was in there with Sienna and he wanted so much to be with them. He wanted to comfort Bella and to keep her calm—well, as calm as she could be with her daughter in the hospital.

His phone rang and he took it out and answered

quickly. The hospital waiting area was quiet and he didn't want to disturb the silence. "Yep," he whispered.

"It's Coop. How's the baby?"

"She's in with the doctor now. Lauren saved the day, I think. Bella didn't know what to do and neither did I. But the steam seemed to work. Sienna's breathing was pretty good by the time we got here. Good thing, too. Bella was frantic."

"I can imagine. That sweet baby is all she has."

Jared took exception to that. She *had* him. Only he'd never told her. He'd never said the things nearest to his heart. That she'd helped him overcome his trust issues. That she was all the woman he would ever want in his life. That he was a goner when it came to Bella Reid.

He loved her.

Grateful he was alone in the waiting room, he grinned like a silly fool just thinking how hard he'd fallen for her. And how, because of her, everything else in his life seemed to fall into place, too. He had to tell Bella he loved her. But now wasn't the time. She was distraught over her daughter's illness, and he couldn't blame her. Sienna was a special kid.

"Hey, you still there?"

"I'm here, Coop."

"It was all I could do to keep Lauren from running out in the middle of the night to meet you at the hospital. Will you talk to her? Assure her about Sienna?"

"Sure, no problem."

"Hi, Jared," Lauren said. "Nurse Lauren needs to know how the patient is doing."

"Well, Nurse Lauren, according to the initial diagnosis, you were right. Sienna has croup. Bella is in with her now."

"They'll give her something to reduce the swelling in her throat. She'll probably stay overnight, just because of her age and the late hour. I would've met you there, but Cooper is being overprotective of me right now."

"As he should be."

"I'm glad you were there with her, Jared. Bella must've been so scared."

"Yeah, she was." So was he. But she'd turned to him for help and the significance of that pumped him up.

The exam room door opened and Bella walked out. "I gotta go, Lauren. Thanks again."

"Of course. Give the baby a hug for me."

"I'll be sure to."

Jared hung up and stood to greet Bella. "How is she?"

"She's sleeping. The doctor says she's going to be fine. The swelling is down now. And they're giving me some medication for her. I only came out to tell you they're keeping her overnight. You don't have to stay. I can—"

"I'm staying, Bella."

When he expected an argument, she slumped into his arms. "Thank you," she whispered.

"Come here, take a rest. You're exhausted." He led her over to a chair and they both took a seat. Wrapping her snugly in his embrace, he kissed her forehead and stroked her arms up and down.

"That feels good," she said softly.

"Feels good to me, too."

She chuckled and a soft glow lit her eyes. "You're so bad."

"You like me that way."

Slowly her eyes closed and she nestled closer into his chest. "I like you any way I can get you."

Jared smiled, totally knocked out. She was soft in his arms and smelled like a sugar cookie. He lifted her chin and placed a soft kiss to her lips. "Me, too, Angel. I like you any way I can get you, too."

Ten

Tuesday morning dawned gloomy and gray, with a light drizzle coming down. After growing up in San Francisco, Bella wasn't bothered that much by the lack of sunshine, and especially not today because Sienna was up and happily singing a silly song along with the cartoon characters on her favorite morning show.

The ordeal with Sienna over the weekend had taken a toll on her nerves. She'd never been more frightened in her life. Yesterday they'd stayed in all day and Sienna had recuperated fast, the meds and the nourishment giving her the boost she'd needed to get better. She hoped to high heaven Sienna wouldn't get croup again, but if she ever did, now she knew how to recognize it and what to do about it.

"Are you ready to go downstairs?"

"See Tared?"

"In a little while. We'll make him a nice lunch for when he gets back." Jared had a doctor's appointment early this morning. She hoped he'd get a clean bill of health. Not that he'd observed his doctor's warning about not driving. But Bella had understood his need to take control and help her. She'd actually appreciated his taking her to the hospital. And though he had driven fast, he hadn't broken any speed laws.

"Come on, let's go."

By the time they got downstairs, the rain was coming down hard. "Looks like we're in for a storm, baby."

They entered the kitchen and she spotted a note at her workstation.

I'll be back before noon. See ya then. Love, Jared.

She smiled at his reference to love. Things were happening quickly between them and she wanted to clear the air, to talk to him from the bottom of her heart. She hoped that he would accept her reasons for not telling him the whole truth. To make him see that it wasn't him she didn't trust, but a fear of her father learning her whereabouts that had kept her lips sealed good and tight.

She glanced at the clock. It was almost noon now. "Okay, well, let's get started," she said, rolling up her sleeves and putting her apron on. She set Sienna down in front of her brand-new dollhouse, a gift from Jared, taking up space right next to the kitchen Christmas tree. *Because she's been sick*, he'd explained. He teased Bella that he had an even better gift for her, but she had to wait until Christmas.

As she was putting the finishing touches on a vegetarian chili dish, with enough kick to knock Jared's socks off, she glanced at the clock. It was already half past twelve and no Jared. She checked the messages on her cell. Nothing.

She was about to text him about his delay, a little knot of tension working its way into her system, when she heard his footsteps at the front door.

Thank goodness. He was home. She picked up Sienna and walked to the door. "Let's surprise Jared," she said. She opened the door with a big smile. And came face-to-face with her father.

Oh, no. She froze and then backed away, her mind racing. She could hardly believe her eyes. "What are you doing here?"

"That's a nice greeting for your old man." He appeared every bit as stately and entitled as he'd always been, but there was sadness in his expression and maybe a few more lines around his eyes than she remembered.

"You mean the father who threatened to take my baby away? *That* old man? The man who cut me off and caused me to run away in fear? I don't think you deserve any sort of greeting from me."

"Francesca, please. Do you know what I've gone through looking for you? The least you could do is let me inside. It's brutally cold and I'm getting soaked."

She hesitated, but finally, because they needed to resolve this, she mustered her courage and stepped away, allowing him entrance. She had no right letting a stranger into Jared's house, but what else could she do? Her father wouldn't just go away. She knew him all too well. He'd stake out the house until Jared got home and then cause a big scene.

"How did you find me?"

"I'll tell you later, but first, let me see Sienna." He turned his attention to her baby. "Hello, sweetheart. Grandpa's here now. How pretty you look this morning." He reached for her to ruffle her hair and Bella stepped back. She wouldn't allow him to touch her baby.

He sighed heavily, looking a bit defeated. "I've missed you. In fact, I've missed both of my girls."

A lump formed in Bella's throat. "Marco, what do you want?"

"I want…a chance to speak with you, Francesca. That's all."

She squeezed her eyes closed briefly. "Ten minutes."

She led him into the parlor and offered him a seat.

Keeping a steady hand on Sienna, she lowered herself down at the far end of the sofa facing him.

"You weren't easy to find, Francesca."

"That was the idea."

"Yvonne says I've been overly harsh with you. She says you believed me when I said I'd cut you off."

"Yes, I did believe you. And you did cut me off. You made my life…unbearable," she admitted, her voice sinking. "I just couldn't take it anymore."

"Yvonne told me as much, too. She's been your advocate, Francesca. I know you two never got along."

"You married a woman only ten years older than me. Hardly a mother to me."

He pointed his finger at her. "Nobody could ever replace your mother, you remember that. The truth is," he said, "I never really got over losing your mother and brother. It was very hard on me and I think, in a way, I placed all my hopes and dreams in you. Maybe unfairly."

"Extremely unfairly."

"I felt you were throwing your life away."

"You tried to dictate my life, Father. You told me what school to go to, what boy to date, what man to marry, where I should work, where I should live. I'm twenty-eight years old. While you weren't looking, I grew up, but you never saw that. You never understood me, never supported my passion for cooking and creating. You wanted me in corporate America. That's not me."

His shoulders slumped. "I was doing it for your own good."

"And look how well that turned out."

He blinked, and anger sparked in his eyes. "Francesca."

"No way, Marco. You have no right to be angry. Not after what you put me through. How do you expect me to trust anything you say?"

"I know, you're...right."

"What?"

"I said, you're right. I admit it. I was overbearing. The truth is, I recently had a health scare. My heart was acting up. I'm going to be okay with diet and a change of lifestyle. But you know, that trip to the hospital got me thinking about my life and what's important to me.

Yvonne says I've finally gotten my priorities straight. She's been helping me with my issues.

"Believe me when I say she cares about you. She wants us to be a family. I came to tell you I'd never take Sienna away from you. It was an idle threat, Francesca. You're a good mother and I never meant for any of this to escalate."

"Are you saying it was all your wild temper?"

"I'm saying I was bluffing to get my way. I'm... sorry."

"You're sorry?" She squeezed her eyes closed briefly. "How did you find me?"

"Apparently a Sienna Reid had been in the hospital overnight. I've had a team of detectives checking all the hospitals, making calls all around the country and...well, we got lucky. Not that Sienna being hospitalized is a good thing. But she looks fine now. What was wrong with her?"

"You mean your henchmen didn't find out?"

"Francesca, please. I love my granddaughter."

"She had a breathing problem due to a virus. Her throat swelled up, but she's much better now."

"Croup?" her father asked.

"How did you know?"

"You're forgetting I was a single father for quite a few years. You had a bout or two of it yourself."

Bella stared at him, stunned. She'd never related what she was going through with what he'd gone through when her mother died. Her father had always seemed larger than life to her.

He gazed at his granddaughter and smiled. "She's a

beauty. Just like you, Francesca. I want you both back in my life."

"Things have changed for me, Father."

"I heard you're working here as a chef."

"How did you— Never mind." She didn't want to know the nefarious ways her father found things out. "I am. I have a job and I've been happy here."

"You can be happy in San Francisco, Francesca. Please consider coming home. Christmas won't be the same without you and Sienna."

Bella glanced at her watch. Jared was late, but he'd be returning soon. She didn't want him to find Marco Forte here, not before she had a chance to explain the situation to him. It was time. And she'd promised Veronica she would. "Father, you have to leave. I have...duties."

He frowned and inhaled a breath, giving her a long stare.

She was ready to ask him again but he beat her to it. "Okay... I'll go."

"You will?" She was astonished. Her father usually never backed down. Maybe Yvonne was a better influence on him than she'd ever given her credit for. And maybe, just maybe, that health scare softened up his heart a bit.

"Yes, as long as you promise to call me. We'll talk some more."

"Yes, we'll talk some more. I do promise."

Marco stood and put out his arms. And when she stood her ground, he walked over to her. Again, she'd triumphed. People always catered to him. She'd never seen this side of her father before.

They embraced, the three of them, Sienna breaking out in giggles.

Her father kissed them both on the cheek and then he was gone. Bella stood with Sienna in the living room, dumbfounded, watching his limo pull away. She couldn't believe what had just happened. Had her father really capitulated? Had she just seen a big change in him? He was actually behaving like a caring father. Well, almost. Or was it all part of a grand scheme to get his way? It was hard to place her trust in him, but his tone, the sincerity in his voice and the genuine look in his eyes had swayed her.

Was her life finally turning around? Did she dare hope?

Bella needed a few minutes to absorb all that had just happened with her father. She sat next to Sienna on the floor and watched her daughter touch some of the shiny ornaments on the Christmas tree as a hard steady rain came down outside. "Careful, baby. We don't want to break them."

Just then the front door burst open and Cooper walked inside, bracing Jared with an arm across his shoulder. Jared's leg was dragging behind him and blood dripped down his face. Cooper guided him toward his bedroom. They were both drenched.

"Cooper?" she called as they passed the living room.

"Jared decided to take his bike out in the rain," Cooper said over his shoulder as he continued moving. "The roads were slick and he took a curve too fast."

"I told you why," Jared lashed back. Bella gasped and plucked up Sienna, taking her into the kitchen and handing her a baby cracker. "Here you go, sweetie. Play with your dollhouse and Mommy will be right back."

Bella approached the bedroom and saw Cooper facing Jared, who was half sitting, half leaning against his pillows on the bed. "You get permission from the doctor to drive and your first decision is to hop on your bike in the middle of a storm?"

"It wasn't storming when I left the house," he said through gritted teeth. "What was I supposed to do? Johnna called in a panic. Her dog knocked loose a steel pipe in the barn and it fell on top of him. The dang thing would've crushed Rusty to death if I hadn't gotten there fast enough. I had to take the back road shortcut and that meant taking the Harley."

Cooper closed his eyes and shook his head. "Man, bro. You don't get it. You went out on slick roads and nearly got yourself killed. This is your second crash this month. When are you gonna learn?"

"Don't lecture me, Cooper. I'm gonna be fine."

"Yeah, once again you defied the odds. How many more chances do you think you'll get?"

Bella stepped up then. "Jared, are you all right?"

"I'm just a little banged up. I'll be fine," he assured her.

"Someone should look at your leg." She glanced at his ripped pants. Blood was already drying on the wound.

"I'm bruised. That's all. No big deal," he said.

She walked into the bathroom, soaked a towel with hot water and antiseptic soap and then returned to the bedroom. "Here," she said, handing him the towel. He appeared startled. Did he expect her to nurse his wounds? He could've been killed today. Did the man have a death wish? "For your face. You'll frighten Sienna if she sees you like that."

She glanced around the bedroom, the place where magic happened between them, the place where she'd felt safe and sheltered. But she didn't feel that way anymore. Now, her eyes were open wide, seeing Jared as he really was, perhaps for the first time. The healthy version of Jared Stone was a man who loved to test his limits. He had a garage full of vehicles to pursue his pastime and he'd never tried to hide his true personality from her. In fact, he'd been only too happy to share his love of speed and danger with her.

He'd said it himself. He wanted to live his life fully before time ran out, the way it had for his father. Jared, once free of restrictions and physical limitations, couldn't wait to hop on his motorcycle and race the storm. And she had been too busy falling in love with him to think this through. Now the cold slap of reality hit her hard.

Jared Stone wasn't father material. He wasn't husband material. He was a man who had been kind and caring to her, but that's where it had to end.

Bella had already lost one good man. She couldn't stand to lose another. Not to death. It was too final, too heart-wrenching. And she'd learned one lesson from her father, if only one, and that was she'd never try to change a person who didn't want to change. If this was the way Jared wanted to live his life, she wouldn't stop him.

"Cooper, will you check on Sienna for me? I need to say something to Jared."

"Uh, sure." He gave her a knowing look, bowing his head to her, his eyes seeming to plead with her to be gentle. "Take your time."

Once Cooper left the room, she had Jared's full attention. Her heart pounded in her chest, her eyes stung and the words were hard to come by. "Jared, I'm...sorry. This isn't going to work."

"What isn't?" His hand froze where he'd been cleaning the blood off his face.

"You and me." She managed a tiny smile.

"Bella, you don't know what you're saying."

"I do know what I'm saying. I'm saying...we're over."

"What, because of this?" His voice rose. He tossed the towel aside and stood, but his wounded leg gave way. He collapsed back on the bed.

Her heart bled, seeing him that way. He braced his elbows on the bed and stayed put. "I can't do this again," she said. "I've been down this road before. I've already lost one good man."

"Bella, come on. You're not gonna lose me. I'm here. I'm fine. I couldn't let that dog die."

"But you could've taken your car and driven a little slower. You could've been more cautious with your life. Every time Paul went up in his chopper, I worried. But he was doing his job, supporting his family. It's what he knew. And when he died, I was crushed. He left me a lonely widow with a child to raise on my own. It's taken me a long time to get to this place in my life."

"I'm not going to let you go."

"You can't stop me. I'm not one to criticize anyone's life choices. Lord knows my father did that to me to the point of suffocation. He tried to run my life and take away my own dreams, my own passions. I won't do that to you. No matter how much I care about you, we're not a good fit."

"I say we are."

"No. You're not what Sienna and I need."

His gaze burned right through her. "Not true, Bella. You know how good we are together. All three of us."

Oh, God. His words destroyed her. She wanted to believe him, to trust him, but she had Sienna to think about. She had to protect her from another loss. It was better to end it here and now. "There's more I have to tell you and you'll be less inclined to want me around once you hear it."

"There's nothing you can say—"

"I've been lying to you."

He blinked and gave her a dubious look. "What are you talking about?"

"I promised your mother I would tell you. And I meant to right away, but then Sienna got sick—"

"My mother?" His brows furrowed, his expression growing dim. That and the blood caking on his face made him appear dangerous. He was, to her well-being. "Bella, what does she have to do with this?"

"My name's not Bella. My real name is Francesca Isabella Forte. I'm heiress to the Forte Foods empire. Your mother recognized me. I'd met her once, a long time ago."

"Where?" he demanded.

"In San Francisco…where I grew up. I only came

to Dallas to spend time with my friend Amy. And then I met you."

He pushed a hand through his hair. "I can't believe this."

It killed her to see his utter disappointment, the admiration he held for her rapidly fading. The loss hit her in the pit of her stomach and she felt the blood drain from her face. How would she ever get over Jared Stone?

She went on to explain. "I'm estranged from my father, and I've been…I've been hiding out here at Stone Ridge Ranch. Trying to make a new start."

His eyes shot fully open. "So you've been lying to me about everything?"

"I'm terribly sorry, Jared. But my father cut me off, or so I thought, and I needed to—"

He stood now, on his own. Pain lined his face and she cringed. He could barely hold himself up, yet he remained standing, favoring his wounded leg. "You needed what? To lie and deceive me? Give me a run for my money? Oh, no, maybe not that. Since you're loaded," he said, raising his voice. "Here I thought I was giving you a home, a job, a place to raise Sienna and all the while…what? You were playing a sick game with me."

"No, it's nothing like that. It's about Sienna. I really thought she was in danger."

"From who?"

"My father. He threatened to take her away from me, to sue me for custody. I panicked and ran. I've been through a lot this past year and I—"

Jared stared at her and began shaking his head. "Are you really a widow?"

"God yes, I wouldn't lie about something like that. Everything I told you about my life before was true."

"You lied about everything else. You didn't trust me. You didn't tell me the truth. And you know how much I *hate* liars."

A shudder ran through her. He was comparing her to Helene, a woman who'd broken his heart and made him wary and closed off. Now he equated her with that awful, cheating woman.

Her emotions high, tears spilled down her cheeks. She never wanted to hurt Jared. She still loved him, but now, even friendship would be too much to ask of him. "I…I couldn't take the risk."

"I'll never be able to trust you." His eyes grew cold, hard. She'd never seen that look on his face before. "I thought you were perfect. My perfect angel."

She didn't have to say she wasn't. That had become abundantly clear.

"You saved my life and I'll always be grateful…" His voice trailed off and he fell back onto the bed, his shoulders slumped. "We were never meant to be."

"No, I know that now. But, Jared, I really didn't want it to end this way. I had planned to tell you the truth."

He snorted in disbelief.

"I really did." Her daughter was her primary concern, and she couldn't subject Sienna to Jared's reckless ways. Even if he could ever forgive her, they wouldn't work. They wanted different things in life. Heartbroken, she had to face facts.

There was no way back from this.

Dread pulsed in the pit of her stomach. "I guess we'll be moving out."

He put his head down and nodded. "Do you have a place, *Francesca*?"

Hearing her real name fall from his lips stymied her. She prayed for strength. "I don't know what I'll do, but I have to go back to San Francisco. I can't hide away any longer. I have to make some hard decisions."

He nodded again. "I'm only concerned for Sienna's sake," he said, unable to hide his bitterness. "I'd like to say goodbye to her."

A lump formed in her throat. "Of course."

She stared at him for a long while. He refused to meet her eyes. There was nothing left between them, and it hurt like hell to admit it. "I'm terribly sorry," she repeated. "Goodbye, Jared."

He said nothing as she walked out of the room.

A loud crashing sound startled her. It was glass breaking against a wall. Jared's vivid curses reached her ears.

She cringed but kept on walking, putting one foot in front of the other, feeling just as shattered as the lamp Jared had just destroyed.

Bella glanced out the study window at her father's mansion. The day was gloomy and gray, matching her mood. Christmas was three days away, but she wished like crazy it would be over already. She put on a happy face for Sienna, making a big deal about her "gampa's"

Christmas tree, all snowy white and flushed with beautifully wrapped presents underneath.

She'd agreed to spend the holidays with her father and that they'd mutually try to patch up their differences. After that, she intended to find a place of her own.

Poor Sienna was confused. She'd settled in nicely at the ranch and though they'd only lived there a few weeks she still mentioned "Tared" often.

And it broke Bella's heart.

She still remembered Jared's near tearful goodbye to Sienna. He'd given her her Christmas gift early, a stuffed toy palomino horse with a thick golden mane and a saddle. Sienna slept with the darn thing at night.

Now they were back in Pacific Heights, yet her heart was in Texas with a handsome rancher with dark blond hair and incredible blue eyes.

"How're you doing?" Yvonne said, coming into the room.

"I'm…okay."

Yvonne glanced at the papers strewed around her desk. "You're still at it? I'm glad to see you haven't given up on your dream."

"Thanks, Yvonne." They'd had a nice long conversation the other day and cleared the air. Yvonne wasn't a threat to her, as Bella had once believed. She was in her corner, and Bella found she'd been overly hard on her father's wife over the years. She'd apologized, hoping it was enough. Yvonne had a good heart. "I'd go crazy if I didn't have something to do right now."

"Marco says tomorrow he's taking you out to look for a place to lease…for your restaurant."

"Yes, he is. He's actually being quite good about it. But I doubt we'll have much luck, being so close to the holiday and all. People have other things on their mind." Now that her trust fund was available to her, she had the resources to pursue her dream.

"I can see that you do."

"I do. It's just that… I'm not sure of anything anymore. I've been going over my recipes and all. But am I ready to open up my own restaurant? I doubt it."

"You're hurting, Francesca."

"Yes." She wasn't going to deny it. Yvonne now knew everything. "It was hopeless from the start, but I can't deny my feelings. I'm in love."

"Nothing's hopeless when there's love involved."

She shrugged. "Jared was furious with me. He practically kicked me out of his house."

"After you broke up with him."

"I know. I did. But…but…"

"You know you can try to speak to him. See if he's cooled down yet."

"No, I can't. He's not a good fit for me. I need stability in my life. I need a man I can count on. I told you about the incident with Jared taking Sienna on that horse. It shaved years off my life seeing Sienna so frightened. No, Jared and I are too different. We want different things in life."

Yvonne took her hand and squeezed. "I think you'll find a way. You're strong, Francesca. Just like someone else I know."

Bella smiled. Maybe Yvonne, with the shapely figure and long blond hair, wasn't a mother figure to her, but they could be friends, and that went a long way in making her feel better. "Thanks. I want to make this a good holiday for Sienna. I'm trying…"

Jared sat in the great room in Cooper's house, watching a football game. Lauren had taken pity on him and invited him over to dinner. His face was a mess, but he'd let his beard grow to hide the scrapes. His leg still ached like a son of a bitch from his most recent crash. But nothing compared to the emptiness in his heart. He was hollowed out inside and pretty bad company.

Lauren sat next to him, offering him a plate of homemade cookies, while Cooper helped Marie with the dishes.

"No thanks," Jared said.

"Hey, when a pregnant woman works all afternoon baking, you need to humor her."

"Okay. Thanks," he said, grabbing one chocolate-chunk cookie. His appetite lately was on the blink. He wanted a Bella-original meal and every time he would think it, he'd cuss himself out for being a fool. If only he could stop thinking about her. Bella, Francesca, whatever the hell she was calling herself lately.

"Coercing you into eating a cookie wasn't the reason I invited you over," Lauren said. "I have news."

"What kind of news?"

"Bella called me. We had a long talk. She's concerned about you. Wanted to know how you were feeling."

"Like crap. But she doesn't need to know that. I'm...
not interested."

"You don't want to know what she had to say?"

"No."

"She put Sienna on the phone and she asked for
Tared."

Jared's eyes squeezed shut. He was on his third bottle
of beer and ready to gulp down the whole damn six-
pack. "That's hitting below the belt."

"Yeah, a real sucker punch to your gut. I'm that good."

Jared eyed his sister-in-law. "And I thought you liked
me."

"I do. I want you to be happy."

"I can't get over how she deceived me, Lauren. It's
like déjà vu all over again. But I thought Bella was
different. I called her my angel. I thought...we had a
chance."

"She is different. Think about this. She didn't deceive you to cause you harm. She didn't want anything
from you. She actually had to be talked into taking the
job. With her father threatening to sue her for custody,
her back was up against the wall. Can you imagine how
frightened she was? Marco Forte is a powerful man and
she didn't know who to trust. She was protecting Sienna. I can understand that. I haven't met my baby yet,
but I'm already a protective mama bear when it comes
to my child." Lauren put her hand on her baby bump.
"There isn't anything I wouldn't do for the ones I love."

"It doesn't matter anyway. She doesn't approve of me."

Lauren laughed, a hearty chuckle that rankled his
nerves. "I can't blame her for that. We're all down on

your hobby. Why can't you just build things, like Cooper does?"

"I'm not Cooper, that's why."

"But you're not stupid, either."

"I'm not too sure about that," Cooper said, walking in and handing him another beer.

"Shut the f- up, Coop."

Lauren shook her head. "Cooper you're not helping."

His brother plunked down on a chair and faced his wife. "Did you ask him yet?"

"I haven't gotten to that," Lauren answered.

"Gotten to what?" Jared asked.

"To asking if you're in love with Bella. Because Lauren is sure she's in love with you."

"Cooper!" Lauren shot Coop a hot glare.

"God, you two. Of course I love her. Why else would I be so damn—"

"Idiotic?" Cooper's brows lifted.

"Hurt?" Lauren suggested.

"Pissed off. Yeah, I'm pissed off, because…damn it. She broke up with me and left."

"You didn't stop her."

"How could I? She betrayed me."

"That again," Cooper grumbled.

"If you really believe she betrayed you, then there's no sense talking any more about it," Lauren said. "But if there's wiggle room inside your head, maybe you should rethink it."

That's all he had been doing lately…thinking. God, he missed Bella and that kid of hers. His house was like a morgue and it'd only been a few days.

Cooper's cell phone rang and he answered it. "Hi, Mom."

Jared began shaking his head. He didn't need a tongue-lashing from his mother tonight. But Cooper looked straight at him and smiled. "Yeah, he's right here." He tossed him the phone. "Mom wants to talk to you."

Jared mouthed a curse at Coop and then answered the phone. He was in for it. His mother wouldn't mince words. She'd been on his case since the first accident. It didn't matter that he was a grown man, worth millions, he was still her little boy worthy of a scolding. Crap. He got up from the sofa and walked out of the room. Seeing his brother gloating was too damn much to take right now.

An hour later, after downing two cups of coffee at Coop's house, Jared drove home at a snail's pace, needing the time to gather his thoughts. When he pulled into the garage, he cut the engine on his Jeep and sat there. Thinking. Special white-tile flooring and all the tools he'd ever need to work on his cars made this a very special place. His vehicles had all the bells and whistles, the finest money could buy. Though his Harley was being repaired and his Lamborghini was gone, all the rest of his collection shone sterling-bright, beckoning him to take them out.

Pick me and I'll give you the thrill of your life.

His phone rang. It was Blake again, manager of his speedboat race team, and Jared knew what he wanted.

It was time to pay the entry fees for the upcoming spring races.

Jared let the call go to voice mail for the third time today.

Then an idea popped into his head and he strode over to his hot red Corvette.

Bella finished wrapping Sienna's final Christmas present and hid it in her bedroom closet. Her daughter understood that Santa would be arriving first thing tomorrow morning, with his special gifts to her, as much as a twenty-three-month-old child could understand. Yet she delighted in the spirit of the holiday, the decorations, the holly and a Christmas tree with lights that changed colors with the click of a remote control.

Bella and Yvonne baked cookies and fudge with Sienna's help. Her daughter mostly licked the spoons and grinned like a monkey afterward. Seeing Sienna enjoy herself so much, a tiny bit of holiday cheer seeped into Bella. Things weren't perfect, but her father had really come around and, for now, she would take it as a small miracle.

Bella descended the stairs and found her father in the parlor, playing blocks on the floor with Sienna. Yvonne had just come in holding a wrapped Christmas box. "This was just delivered. It's something for you, Francesca." She handed her the box.

"Thanks."

She sat on the sofa and turned the box around on all sides, shaking it a bit, curious who had sent it. She lifted the lid carefully and moved the wrapping paper aside.

A copy of the *Dallas Tribune* was inside. She shook her head and lifted it out. "See Page Three" was written diagonally across the front page in big, bold letters.

"What is this?" she muttered, turning the pages. And then she found the headline: Dallas Tycoon Jared Stone's Charity Auction.

She blinked, her hands trembling. She continued to read on.

"What is it?" Yvonne asked after a few impatient moments.

"It's an article about how Jared is auctioning off all his cars and motorcycles and will be developing a new foundation to benefit children's causes. All of the proceeds of the auction will go to the foundation."

Bella continued reading and then she gasped. "Oh!"

"What is it?" Yvonne asked. Her father's eyes were on her, too.

"Jared's naming the new f-foundation…" Bella choked up, unable to speak for a second. She held back tears. "He's naming it…Sienna's Hope."

"Sounds like the man's got some smarts after all," her father said.

"That's…amazing, Francesca." Yvonne smiled. Then she glanced at Marco and the two seemed to have some secret communication.

"What?" Bella asked, still shaking.

"There's another gift waiting for you and Sienna outside."

Emotions roiled in the pit of her stomach. "There is?"

"Yes, and it's pretty cold out there, so put on your coats and hurry."

"What's going on?" Obviously it was something Yvonne and Marco were privy to.

"Christmas comes early sometimes," Yvonne said, ushering her into her coat while her father put on Sienna's quilted jacket.

They nearly shoved her out the front door. She glanced back and Yvonne grinned and shut the door in her face. Bella took Sienna's hand. "Apparently, little one, there's a surprise waiting for us out here."

She climbed down the steps and walked along the path leading to the front gate.

Outside her father's house stood a living, breathing Jared Stone next to a pearl-white SUV.

Her heart pounding in her ears, she absorbed the sight of him. Oh, how she'd missed him. Before she could utter a word, Sienna let go of her hand. "Tared!" She raced toward him and lifted her arms. "Up."

"Hello, little angel." He picked her up and kissed her cheek. It was a solid sight, the two of them together. It seemed so right.

Bella walked up to him. "Jared?"

He set Sienna down and immediately came closer to graze her cheek with the palm of his hand. It was cold outside, yet the contact sizzled, warming her up inside. Was she silly to hope?

"God, you're beautiful. I've missed you like crazy, Bella."

"I've missed you, too. But what are you doing here?"

"I came for you," he said as naturally as breathing. "I realized once you left, nothing much mattered to me. I don't need to catch up to life. Or race toward it. I need a life. With you."

"So…you've forgiven me for lying to you?" This was all so unbelievable. More than she could've ever imagined, but she had to ask.

"Let's say I understand why you did it now, Bella. I can't fault you for wanting to protect little Sienna. I just wish you'd trusted me."

"Oh, Jared. If I could do it all over again, I would. I know the kind of man you are. You would've protected us. And what you did, naming your foundation after Sienna, just about destroyed me. It was incredible and thoughtful. It means so much to me."

He took her hand and held it tight. "I'm glad it made you happy. That's all I want to do. I love you, Bella. You *are* my angel. No matter what, I don't want to live without you. I've given up my race cars for this. There's a car seat already installed."

Tears rimmed her eyes as she gazed at the SUV. "There is?"

He nodded.

"And you won't be sorry later?" she asked.

"No, never. I've realized how that part of my life is over, Bella. I'm gonna live my life in the present and not try to outrace the future. I swear to you. I only want you and Sienna in my life. The two of you are all I need. I called and explained that to your father and his wife. I think they know I only want your happiness."

Jared and her father had spoken? She was a little stunned. "And Father…agreed?"

"He wasn't thrilled, but yes, in the end, he wants what's best for you."

"I love you, Jared. And you're all I need, too."

"You do? You love me?" He grinned, a daring, blue-eyed pirate's grin. How could she have ever thought of living without this man?

"Will you come home to the ranch with me, Bella? Be my wife?"

"You're asking me to marry you?"

He nodded. "Will you, Bella?"

Joy consumed her. She had no doubts anymore. "Jared, yes. Yes. I'll be your wife."

His mouth came down on hers in a fiery all-consuming kiss and she moaned from the sheer pleasure. Oh, how she'd missed him. How she couldn't wait to marry him.

"Best Christmas present ever," he whispered and then lifted Sienna up again, the three of them huddling together.

"For me, too," she said, squeezing him tight.

He pulled away slightly to look into her eyes. "Bella, I don't want you to give up on your dreams. If you want to write a cookbook or open a restaurant, I'll support your decision."

"You will?" She beamed inside. Jared would always be by her side. And she wanted to do both, but not right now. Now she just wanted to go home to Stone Ridge. "You mean you'll still let me experiment on you with my new recipes?"

"Are you kidding? Secretly meeting up with the Midnight Contessa is the favorite part of my day. I look forward to it."

She laughed. "Me, too."

Those late-night encounters with Jared were scorching hot. She couldn't wait until they could be together that way again, meshing their bodies, melding their minds, making incredible love.

"Promise me one thing, Bella. You'll always be my own personal chef."

"Always, my love."

It would be an easy promise to keep.

* * * * *

If you liked this story of an alpha hero tamed by love—and a baby—
don't miss the next
Billionaires and Babies story:

Keeping Secrets
by Fiona Brand
Available September 2018!

Or any of these other
Billionaires and Babies stories:

His Accidental Heir *by Joanne Rock*
The CEO's Nanny Affair *by Joss Wood*
The Christmas Baby Bonus *by USA TODAY*
bestselling author Yvonne Lindsay
Taming the Texan *by Jules Bennett*

***

If you're on Twitter, tell us what you think of
Harlequin Desire! #harlequindesire

Get 4 FREE REWARDS!

We'll send you 2 FREE Books plus 2 FREE Mystery Gifts.

Harlequin® Desire books feature heroes who have it all: wealth, status, incredible good looks... everything but the right woman.

FREE
Value Over
$20

*When Caleb attends a colleague's wedding, the last
person he expects to leave with is the runaway bride!
He offers Shelby a temporary hideout on his ranch. But
soon the sizzle between them has this wealthy cowboy
wondering if seduction will convince her to stay…*

Read on for a sneak peek of
Runaway Temptation
by USA TODAY *bestselling author Maureen Child,
the first in the Texas Cattleman's Club:
Bachelor Auction series!*

Shelby Arthur stared at her own reflection and hardly
recognized herself. She supposed all brides felt like
that on their wedding day, but for her, the effect was
terrifying.

She was looking at a stranger wearing an old-fashioned
gown with long, lacy sleeves, a cinched waist and full
skirt, and a neckline that was so high she felt as if she
were choking. Shelby was about to get married in a dress
she hated, a veil she didn't want, to a man she wasn't sure
she liked, much less loved. How did she get to this point?

"Oh, God. What am I doing?"

She'd left her home in Chicago to marry Jared
Goodman. But now that he was home in Texas, under
his awful father's thumb, Jared was someone she didn't

even know. Her whirlwind romance had morphed into a nightmare and now she was trapped.

Shelby met her own eyes in the mirror and read the desperation there. In a burst of fury, she ripped her veil off her face. Then, blowing a stray auburn lock from her forehead, she gathered up the skirt of the voluminous gown in both arms and hurried down the hall and toward the nearest exit.

And ran smack into a brick wall.

Well, that was what it felt like.

A tall, gorgeous brick wall who grabbed her upper arms to steady her, then smiled down at her with humor in his eyes. He had enough sex appeal to light up the city of Houston, and the heat from his hands, sliding down her body, made everything inside her jolt into life.

"Aren't you headed the wrong way?" he asked, and the soft drawl in his deep voice awakened a single thought in her mind.

Oh, boy.

Don't miss
Runaway Temptation
by USA TODAY *bestselling author Maureen Child,
the first in the Texas Cattleman's Club:
Bachelor Auction series.*

*Available September 2018 wherever
Harlequin® Desire books and ebooks are sold.*

www.Harlequin.com

HDEXP0818

LOVE
Harlequin
romance?

Join our Harlequin community to share your thoughts and connect with other romance readers!

Be the first to find out about promotions, news, and exclusive content!

Sign up for the Harlequin e-newsletter and download a free book from any series at
www.TryHarlequin.com

CONNECT WITH US AT:

Harlequin.com/Community

 Facebook.com/HarlequinBooks

 Twitter.com/HarlequinBooks

 Instagram.com/HarlequinBooks

 Pinterest.com/HarlequinBooks

ReaderService.com

 **HARLEQUIN**®

**ROMANCE WHEN
YOU NEED IT**

HSOCIAL2017